I0633024

A TANGLED WEB OF FRONTIER LIFE

BROOKSIDE, OREGON TERRITORY BOOK ONE

JOHNNY GUNN

WOLFPACK
PUBLISHING
— EST 2013 —

A Tangled Web of Frontier Life
Paperback Edition
© Copyright 2022 Johnny Gunn

Wolfpack Publishing
5130 S. Fort Apache Rd. 215-380
Las Vegas, NV 89148

wolfpackpublishing.com

Paperback ISBN 978-1-63977-499-9
eBook ISBN 978-1-63977-300-8
LCCN 2021952833

A TANGLED WEB OF FRONTIER LIFE

"I tell you, Martha, this has been the worst year ever. I thought last year was bad, but those late summer rains, snow as deep as the eves all winter, the springtime freezes, and then losing little Katherine, I don't think I can take much more." Jacob Hoagland was thirty years old and had moved to the valley five years before with his young wife, Martha, and their two-year-old son, Lucas. Katherine was born the year after their arrival and had been sickly from birth, finally passing on in mid-July.

"All the good words the good people showered on us," he stammered, "rolled off like the summer rain. Who can put into words the loss of a child? I can fix the irrigation ditches, replant the trees, fix things that are broken, but I can't undo that incredible loss." They were seated at their kitchen table, made of fine Oregon fir, having a mid-afternoon coffee.

Jacob was a farmer, a craftsman, and, to a degree, an optimist most of the time. He knew that table he'd made would be in the family for a hundred years. The Hoagland farm, despite the problems is a big producer and the family eats well, sleeps warm, and is well respected in the valley. Eighteen-Forty-Seven was not a good year for many in the valley, not just the Hoagland's.

"Katherine can never be with us again, Jacob, but more children can be," Martha said. "You are a natural father. Have I ever told you that? From the day you introduced yourself to Lucas, all bloody and screaming at the top of his lungs, you have been a father in the best description of the word. We'll have more children, and we'll always have Katherine's memories, as short as they are."

It was early December, 1847, and the Hoagland family homestead stood in the rolling foothill country in the far north of Oregon's Willamette Valley. It stood in what Jacob considered, ruins. "I'm about ready to call it quits and move to California and see if we can find some of that good ground everyone's talking about." He had a wry, almost ironic, grin on his face. "Except I love Oregon."

"You're a farmer, Jacob, as your father was and his father before him. You're the strongest, bravest man I've ever known, and I really don't think you would quit what we've spent so many years building. We found one hundred and sixty acres of trees and brush and rocks, Jacob, and you turned that into rolling fields of grain and grass. You turned hillsides of rock into pastures now filled with sheep and cattle, and you turned this little meadow we're in, into a homesite filled with warmth and love.

"No, Jacob, you aren't going to quit and neither am I." Martha was five years younger than Jacob, was schooled in Philadelphia and met Jacob Hoagland while on a family trip to St. Louis. Hoagland was a strapping young man helping to organize a wagon train to Oregon. He and four other men had filed on frontier land and were gathering others to join their party. It wasn't really love at first sight, but close when Jacob saw Martha in the dry goods store one afternoon.

"Would this be strong enough material for a shirt when I reach Oregon?" He asked the lady behind the glass counter. Martha, shopping with a friend walked over and picked up the bolt of cloth.

"My heavens, no," she said. Her eyes were intense as she put the bolt back in place and brought another one out. "As big and strong as you are, you're probably hard on good twill. This would be far better for a man like you."

That conversation extended into a brief stop for coffee and pie, and then supper at Martha's friend's house. The whirlwind romance culminated in marriage within the month, and young Lucas was born ten months after that. The argonauts left for their cross-continent adventure within weeks of Lucas's arrival.

"You fought savages, killed game, built boats, doctored sick and wounded, Jacob, all across this vast place we call the United States, and I know you are not a quitter." Martha was a dark haired, dark eyed beautiful young woman who carried her baby while working in the fields alongside her husband. She loaded one flint-lock while Jacob aimed and fired the other when savages were out to kill them. She turned the stone and sharpened axes so Jacob could fell timber and milked her kitchen cow twice a day.

He took her hand and they walked out of the kitchen. "It's winter, Martha, and I'm not even cold today. Being able to spend hours like this with you is what I live for every day I start work." He picked up a rock and sailed it out into the meadow.

"Maybe these hours and those when there is no light, and we're between the blankets."

She giggled, picked up a rock and threw it even farther out than he had. He looked at her, laughed, picked up a larger rock and arced it far into the deep grasses, not winter brown. Martha laughed again, and walked on, giving him the win.

Martha was tall and wiry, tough on the outside and a true romantic on the inside. The warmth and love she shared with her family often splashed over to their friends as well. "We have the winter to rebuild those irrigation ditches. We have plenty of seed for spring planting, and we didn't lose the fruit trees. We certainly won't starve, with cattle, sheep, hogs, chickens, and game."

Jacob looked across at the large meadow where they were standing and gathered his wife in his strong arms. "You're right, my lady, I'm not a quitter. I'm beat down, bruised and hurt, but I'm not broken, and we will make this place green and growing again." His green eyes burned their love into her big brown eyes, and there would be the possibility of another child coming along soon, if they stayed out there much longer.

They walked the half mile through winter brown grass toward the rambling farmhouse Jacob had built during their first year on the homestead. "Strange, isn't it, that winter is the easiest of the seasons to get along with? We can prepare for the brutal cold, high winds, and heavy precipitation.

"It's the spring and summer that mess with us. Plant your crop and when it sprouts, old Jack Frost nips those little buds. Let your crop get growing well and heavy rains wash it away. But winter? We know old man winter is out to do us in." He had to chuckle as he talked, knowing the irony of what he was saying had so much truth to it.

As they neared the big farmhouse, Luke came running to meet them. "Papa, Papa," he cried, and jumped into Jacob's arms. "It's cold."

"Winter's here, son. Time to put away the short pants, I'm afraid. We'll have snow on the ground soon."

"I like snow," Luke said. "We'll build a big old snowman again, won't we? That was sure a big one last year."

"It sure was," Jacob laughed remembering how he and Luke had used shovels to make a snowman that stood almost six feet high. Lucas had a miniature of Jacob's shovel and could throw snow almost to the top of their big man. "Let's use a turnip for the nose this year."

Squeals of joy from the boy led the family up the kitchen steps and into the cabin. The house was warm when they went in through the kitchen door and Jacob added wood to the cook stove and to the fireplace in the great room. "We'll see snow before the week is out, I think."

"I have a Dutch oven filled with lamb stew for our dinner, boys," Martha said. "A platter of buttermilk biscuits to sop it up with and peach cobbler for dessert. That'll warm us up."

Bowls filled with fine food and there wasn't much talk around the table until after the cobbler disappeared. "I sure would like a pony all my own for Christmas," Luke said. "I like old Jasper the plow horse, but he's not really mine. I want my own, a pinto pony." He was jumping up and down, laughing with the thought.

The joy left Jacob's face as he listened to his son. There weren't many coins in the tin breadbox, and he didn't have much corn, wheat, and squash to use for trading. There wasn't going to be much of a Christmas around the Hoagland farm this year he thought. He looked over and saw Martha try her best to look away. This is when it's hard to be the man of the house, Jacob thought, to provide. It was at times like this that memories of his family and their farms back east flooded his thoughts.

His father, Orson, was a provider, and his grandfather, Lucas, as well. They settled in the wilds of the Ohio Valley back when it was the frontier. Did Old Lucas face these kinds of ordeals from Orson? Did Orson face them from him? "My God, little Luke, I'm not sure about that. A pony, eh?" Jacob said. Martha smiled and went to the stove for the coffee pot.

"Never did have one of my own when I was growing up," he said. "We had mules when I was a boy in the Ohio Valley. Only one of them would let me ride him, but we did go places. Kind of like the way you and Jasper do."

"Yeah," Lucas said. He was laughing. "Didn't you want a pony, though, even though you had a mule to ride?"

"I had three brothers and five sisters, Luke, and pa had his brother's family living with us, too. Uncle Bart was dead of the flu, and his wife and four kids lived with us. There weren't a nickel's worth of spending money in a month's time, boy. We ate good, like we do here, but as for finding some silver to spend, it weren't there."

Is this boy of mine too young to understand when I talk about our money situation? Was I able to understand what my father talked about? I must have been. Must have, because it seems I've known how to make what little coin we have work for us. Luke is a strong and intelligent boy. He'll understand.

Luke sat back in his chair, sniffled just a little bit, wiped his nose on his sleeve, and looked at his mother.

"What pa's trying to say, mama, is that I ain't gonna get a pony for Christmas, ain't he?"

"It sounded that way to me." She couldn't hold back the gentle laugh. It always surprised her when this little boy sounded so much like an adult. "Your pa's a pretty special man, Luke, and he wouldn't ever not take care of us. We may not get some of the things we want but we'll never go hungry or die of the cold, as long as Mr. Hoagland is around."

"What I really want is a brother, mama. You don't have to buy them, do you?"

Jake Hoagland couldn't hold the laugh in at all, almost spat out his coffee, and roared it out across the table. "I guess you got me on that one, son. Mrs. Hoagland, Ma'am, do you think we can work on that?"

"I'll check the calendar, sir," she chuckled. "Why don't you gentlemen go sit by the fire while I clean up around here." Jacob saw the tinge of pink in her cheeks and the way she tried to hide her sly grin. She looked away before continuing. "Would you like a brandy, Jacob? And, maybe an oatmeal cookie for you, young man?"

Jake sat in his rocking chair, Luke in his little boy's rocker, both built by Jacob, and enjoyed their after supper treats. *I don't have any idea where I might come up with enough money to get that scamp a good riding horse. I couldn't come up with ten dollars cash right now no matter how hard I tried. Martha's right, though. We won't starve or freeze to death. I like the idea of more babies, though. I really do.*

"THAT BOY'S PUT ME IN A PICKLE JAR, MARTHA. I CAN'T get him that pony." They were under a heavy wool blanket watching the flicker of flame and shadows

7

thrown around the room from their bedroom Ben Franklyn fireplace.

"There was a second request," she giggled.

"That I'm about to work on," he said and pulled her close. "Come spring I think I'll plant some cash crops. People in towns have to eat, too, you know." She snuggled up close to the big man and nibbled gently on an ear.

CHAPTER 2

The first of winter's heavy storms roared down the Willamette River Valley on December 20th and laid a blanket of snow about a foot deep on the Hoagland property. "You have that entire shed filled with wood, Jacob, the meat barrels are salted and brined, and grass is cut for the animals. Come in, now, and sit by the fire." She gently looked at his big rocker and gestured that he sit. "Our boy is going to get his second wish."

Her eyes were soft, and the smile was as warm as summer's sun. "Wonderful," Jacob whispered. "A late summer baby will make the summer miserable for you, I'm afraid. What will it be? A boy? A girl?"

"One of each," she giggled. "I might miss the harvest, but you've always done that by yourself. Lucas is getting big enough to help, too. When the snow melts, will there be more run-off damage?"

"Not like a rain does. I did a lot of earth moving, so we won't face those problems. I want to expand your kitchen garden, Martha, and make it a cash crop garden. Can you and Luke make that work? Sure would be a big help."

"You brought that up at supper sometime back and I'm already planning for it. I've talked to neighbors and the village people too, and I think it's a good idea."

"Zeb came by this afternoon while I was stacking that last cord of wood." Jacob said. He had a half smile on his face. "Says he's gonna pull out come spring and is putting his place up."

"Oh, my," she said. "After all that work. Poor man." She was standing behind his chair and rubbed his shoulders and neck. "What a loss for him."

"Says he's going south to California. Just going to walk out and leave everything. Wants me to come by and take what I want before he pulls out."

"All that farm machinery? Those plows and … Everything?"

"That's what he says. I'm going into the village tomorrow and talk with Eb Creighton at the land office, see if I can absorb some of that bottom land of Zeb's. He's only been on that land two years, Martha. He hasn't fulfilled his five years. He doesn't have anything to sell."

"Poor man. All that work, all those expenses."

"He just wasn't that smart, honey. Instead of making do, he spent all his money on those fancy plows and machinery, and then we've had this miserable year and he wasn't ready for it. He doesn't have much stock, didn't do enough planning. It's a shame. At least he isn't married, doesn't have children. He'll survive."

FOR MANY PEOPLE, LIFE ON THE FRONTIER WASN'T A HIT OR miss situation. Just getting to a place like Brookside, Oregon Territory in the late 1840s was an ordeal that many would not survive. Those that did were tough, raw-boned, and independent. Brookside was filled with them.

The village itself sat in the flat lands along the mighty Willamette, its muddy streets lined with a combination of private homes, businesses, even home/offices. The most active of the businesses served the outlying farms and ranches but there were inns and taverns for the locals and travelers coming through.

Among the more popular inns was Murphy's run by Murphy O'Reilly and his wife. Their stock in trade was an always filled cast iron pot filled with stew. It was home to most of the single loggers who put away vast bowls of the stew late every day of the week. Murphy and the Missus came west as youngsters from Ireland, through the Ohio Valley, and just kept coming, all the way to Oregon Territory.

There were those on the frontier, the same as in the more civilized world, who simply couldn't live by the rules, and thus Brookside had a village constable and a judge appointed by the territorial governor. Constable Tobias Kennedy was a ferocious man straight from the Emerald Isle. Kennedy stood tall at five feet and ten inches, weighed a hefty two hundred pounds, and the only weapon he carried, other than two raw, hard knuckled hands, was an ancient oak walking stick.

The number of bruises, welts, and bumps that hefty piece of heavy wood inflicted was large indeed. Kennedy had a raw sense of humor, allowed for shenanigans that did not involve destruction of property or injury to man or beast. Kennedy never married and there were a few single ladies who did their best to catch his attention.

The territory needed people, the land was rich, and the water was plentiful. Land was available, a hundred and sixty acres at a time and all one had to do was build a home and work the land for five years, after which you had the deed. In Brookside, the land office was run by Edwin Creighton. His official duties often raised eyebrows, but he had never actually been charged with a crime.

J ake had the mules harnessed and Lucas was on the wagon seat next to him for the ride into the little village. "We'll be back before supper, Martha, maybe with some good news for a change." He flicked the mules and they stepped right out. "Gonna be a cold ride, Luke. Keep that blanket wrapped tight."

It was five miles into the little town and man and boy were glad there was no wind blowing. The morning temperature was in single digits and the mules were breaking ice on the road. "Is Mr. Engle selling everything, Pa?"

"Almost giving it away, son. Wants out before the heavy winter sets in. While I'm talking with Mr. Creighton, I want you to stay with his wife. Jeremy's about your age, isn't he?"

"He's older, Pa. He's a bully but not with me. He pushes his sister around but not me. He tried to push me last year and I gave him a bloody nose."

Jacob wanted to laugh but knew he shouldn't. "Fightin' ain't always the best answer, Luke. I don't want you to get the idea that it is. You're a big boy, strong because of our work, but only use that size and strength for good things. Don't you be a bully. You be a gentleman while you're visiting."

"Ma already made me promise," he said, and Jake had to laugh.

"We'll only be about an hour and then we'll ride back to Zeb Engle's place and have a long goodbye with him. Ma packed a good dinner for us, so we'll eat after I meet with the land manager."

EB CREIGHTON WAS NEARING FIFTY YEARS AND WAS married to a much younger woman. They had a daughter and a son named Jeremy. The son was idolized by the older man while the daughter was barely recognized. Jeremy was spoiled rotten, slightly tolerated around the town, and far more than Mrs. Creighton could handle. Creighton held the territorial position of land officer for that county and considered himself somewhat of a big shot.

Creighton's wife was named Irene and they had a son, Jeremy and daughter, Carrie. Mrs. Creighton was seldom seen about the village and when seen, was often sporting bruises. Their family life was discussed by the little old ladies over tea and biscuits.

"So, Engle's giving it up, eh? Serves him right always bragging about his money, his new equipment. Needed to work, not talk," the pompous Creighton said when Jacob Hoagland told him about Engle leaving.

"I'd like to file on that, one hundred acres along the Scudder Creek, Creighton. Engle's homestead is voided now," Jake said. "Engle gave me quite a bit of his equipment and that section bumps right up to my western fields."

14

"These things are always a bit awkward, Hoagland," Creighton said. He was at his large desk in a small room off the living room of his home. "Engle had two years to go on his homestead contract, so, yes, his holdings are voided, and you are certainly eligible to file. The filing fee is two dollars."

Jake handed over two silver dollars trying not to let his face show the gentleman that it was the last two he had. "Come by in a day or two, Hoagland, and you can pick up the papers. Your homestead contract is fulfilled, so this will be a new five-year contract."

They shook hands and Jacob gathered little Luke up and drove the mules out of the town toward Engle's place. "I don't see any open wounds or bruises, Luke. How did your time with Jeremy go?"

"Mrs. Creighton sure is a nice lady, Pa. We had cookies and hot chocolate. Mama makes better cookies, though."

"I'm glad you liked them and hope you thanked her." Luke gave a nod. "Now, about that question?" Jacob wasn't going to let the boy out of answering.

"Well," Lucas stammered, "I didn't have much fun. Jeremy hit his little sister in the head and it really hurt her. Mrs. Creighton wasn't there, and somebody had to do something." Lucas got very serious, sat straight up on the hard buckboard seat, and continued. "I told Jeremy that it was wrong to hit a girl and he should apologize and ask forgiveness."

"What did you do, Luke? You're right, though. It's not gentlemanly to hit girls or women. Not nice at all. Go on." Jacob was sure there would be considerably more to come.

"He called me a sissy and said he could hit his sister

any time he wanted. I told him again it was wrong and, Pa, do you know what he said next?"

"No, Son, I don't. Why don't you tell me?" Jacob was getting a kick out of his son's story and hoped it would end well.

"That Jeremy Creighton said he could hit anyone he wanted, any time he wanted to. He said his father said so. I said it wasn't nice to lie. Isn't that right, Pa?"

"Yes, it is. Go on." Jacob was trying to put it all together and came up with his answer. Little Jeremy probably wasn't lying at all. Ed Creighton was arrogant enough to probably tell his son something like that.

"Well," Lucas said. This was, after all, man to man talk. "He walked right up to me and tried to hit me like he hit his sister. I pushed him back and he fell down. When he got up, he tried to hit me again and I hit him right in the nose. That's when Mrs. Creighton came in. She was really mad at me until Jeremy's sister told her what happened. She's kind of cute when she's angry, Pa."

"Mrs. Engle?" Jacob's turn to sit straight up on the wagon seat. His son thinks Jeremy's mother is kind of cute? *Maybe it's time for that boy and I to have a little talk.*

"No!" Lucas frowned and looked at his father. "Her name is Carrie. That's a nice name."

Jacob chuckled over the story for the rest of the ride. "I think you did the right thing, Son. You defended yourself and defended the honor of a fine lady, too."

Hoagland found a cottonwood tree standing off to the side of road and pulled the wagon under its generous branches. "How about we have something to eat before we meet with Mr. Engle. that is unless you filled up on those cookies."

"I'm hungry, Papa. Mama has some roast beef in that basket. I can already taste it."

16

CHAPTER 4

"Afternoon, Zeb," Jacob said as he pulled the team to a halt. "Looks like you're pretty much packed up."

"Yes, I am," Engle said. "Just not a farmer, Jake. Just not. You had a talk with that big-shot land man? He's probably gonna want to sell this land instead of putting it back on the map. Don't mind telling you, Ed Creighton's a criminal if I ever saw one."

Lucas was off looking at the equipment that now belonged to their farm and Jacob took the opportunity to ask Engle about his mule. "You ride that mule in a saddle, don't you, Zeb?"

"He ain't much for pullin' a plow, Jake, but when we go up in the mountains, he can carry a deer back with no problem, and he's fine riding. Sam Donaldson wants him, but his wife said no, they already had too many mules. Might have been talking about Sam," he laughed. "You want him, Jake? He ain't much good on the farm."

"Don't say anything to Lucas, Zeb. It's for him. He wants a pinto pony, he's gonna have to put up with an old black mule. Martha wants you to swing by our place on your way out, Zeb. She has a half barrel of salted meat and some potatoes and onions for your trip south."

"That's awfully kind of you, Jake. I'm gonna miss you, boy. Should I drop off the mule on my way?"

"No, leave him in your corral there and I'll sneak him home." Jacob took in a long breath hoping he was doing the right thing and wondering about what Engle said about Creighton. "Do you think old Ed Creighton would really try to ace me out of this homestead of yours? I paid the fee for filing and he said it would be treated as a new land agreement, that is, I would have five years to prove it up."

"I don't know what that fool might do, Jake. My only advice to you would be to keep my eyes wide open, my ears free of wax, and my long gun handy. I better keep packing. How you gonna get this equipment over to your place?"

"I'll lead the mules over in the morning behind the wagon and Luke can drive the wagon with extra stuff and follow me as I drive the plows, threshers, cutters, and wagons back, one at a time. Gonna be a two-day job for sure."

"If I had your energy, Jacob Hoagland, I wouldn't be moving to California."

Jacob heard those words over and over as he and Lucas rode back to the Hoagland farm. *He was right is what Martha would say. I would never call the man lazy, but he did make a point there. Now, I got another animal to feed.* He had to chuckle wondering how he would let Lucas know he wasn't getting a pinto pony for Christmas, but an old black mule instead.

. . .

Edwin Creighton sat quietly as his wife told him about how Jeremy had started a fight with Lucas Hoagland. "You believe Carrie before you believe my son?" His anger was slowly building and his wife knew she would probably take the brunt of it when it finally came to the surface. "You let that snot-nosed farmer's son whip on my son? Bring him to me this instant and then remove yourself and your daughter from my sight."

Mrs. Creighton stood near the wood stove and slowly put her hands on her ample hips, glowering. "I'll do no such thing, Ed Creighton. You may get away talking like that to some of the people in this community, but you'll not talk to me that way."

"Now, you listen here, woman. As long as I'm the man of this house you'll do as I say. Get those children in here now." Creighton moved his chair back and grunted loudly, getting to his feet. He took two steps toward Mrs. Creighton and was met with a face full of scalding coffee.

"You'll never lay a hand on me, Ed Creighton. Never again," she screamed. Irene picked up a cast iron frying pan that measured some twelve inches across and swung it with both hands, knocking the rotund gentleman across the kitchen where he stumbled over his chair and fell to the floor, screaming in agony. Blood was pouring from the terrible wound to his head and he was thrashing about in agony from the burns to his face.

The noise brought the children and Irene stood mute when they ran in. "Pa," Jeremy yelled, kneeling next to the man. The pain from the boiling coffee and the extreme head injury had to be agonizing, and Ed Creighton was sobbing. Carrie ran to her mother and hid her face in Irene's apron.

"Go get the doctor Jeremy. Your father is in pain.

Carrie, it's past your bedtime, honey. Remember to brush your teeth." Jeremy grabbed his coat and raced out the kitchen door while Irene, ignoring her whimpering husband, started cleaning up the mess she made with the coffee. "You'll never touch me again, Ed. Never. I'll not let your son grow into your type, either. My father was a gentleman and my son will be, also."

Raised on a sprawling hillside farm in New Hampshire, Irene Fletcher was brought up to be a lady in every way. She idolized her father and styled herself after her mother, a charming New England bred lady. Mr. Fletcher had not fully approved of her marriage to Creighton, believed his daughter was wearing blinders, and was dead set against their move to Oregon Territory.

"My father was right, Ed. You are not a gentleman." She put more wood in the fire and started a fresh pot of coffee. It wasn't long and Jeremy came back with Doctor Ralph Winston. Irene never said a word, just pointed at the injured man, now curled in a fetal position, still whimpering.

"My God, Irene. What happened?" He knelt down and saw the terrible gash in Creighton's head, blood streaming from the wound, and was horrified by the blisters all over Creighton's face. "Irene? Did you …?" He never finished the sentence as he saw her emotionless face nodding gently. "Let's get him into a bed," he said.

"No," Irene said. "He needs to be out of this house. I'll not have him in my bed, I'll not have him in my house."

"I can't move him, Irene. He'll die. His skull is cracked open."

At those words, Jeremy let out a scream and Carrie started crying wildly. Carrie was still holding Irene tight, and Jeremy tried to hug his father, but was pulled back by the doctor. "You children need to go to bed now. Doctor Winslow will take care of your father. Go along now." The two looked at Creighton, then to their mother, and slowly ebbed their way out of the room, both crying, not holding hands.

"This is terrible, Irene. I must get help, and you know, I must report this to the constable."

"You do that, Doctor. This town needs to know what a horrible man Ed Creighton is. I'll have coffee when you bring help." She skirted around the table and sat such that she couldn't see the whimpering Creighton on the floor. "He'll never touch me again," she whispered.

CHAPTER 5

E d Creighton lived another two days with the massive head wound. Doctor Winston was able to hold off infection in the burns to his face, but there was serious brain damage from the cast iron frying pan that couldn't be doctored. Town constable Tobias Kennedy, recently out of Cork, by way of Boston, brought the news to Irene.

"It pains me, Mrs. Creighton, to have to tell you that your husband passed away early this morning. I'm sure you understand that you and I need to have a long conversation." His New England manners fought with the hard truths of the frontier but were welcomed by Irene. Her children were staying with friends, and she was the source of most conversations around Brookside.

"I'm sure the town is enjoying this," she said. Her voice was soft, her eyes almost sparkled as she invited Constable Kennedy to sit down. "Mr. Creighton was not a nice man, to me, to Carrie, or to the many people he had to deal with as the land agent for the government."

"Yes, there have been stories told about. Will you tell

22

me about the night he was so severely injured? Take all the time you need."

"I fear for my children, Tobias. They've never had a real father, and now, Christmas just around the corner, they won't have that either. I'll tell you everything. It will cleanse my soul to do so. Would you like some coffee? I've some fresh biscuits and jam, too."

She started talking, as if to a friend over for a visit, not the town's law enforcement. As she prepared coffee and biscuits for them, she said, "Ed started being mean while we were still on the long road called the Oregon Trail. After Jeremy was born it got worse and worse. Jeremy could do no wrong but Carrie and I could do no right. He felt he had a right to beat me any time he felt like it."

Kennedy had heard the stories and now realized just how true the rumors had been. He nodded, took a bite of biscuit and sip of coffee, not wanting to look into the sad woman's eyes. She was younger than she looked, he realized when he did see her eyes.

"It was horrible, Tobias." She refused to cry or even show an emotion other than that of being beat down for so many years. "That day, when I finally could take it no longer started with a visit by Jacob Hoagland and his son, Lucas."

She had a tub of fresh butter from the well house out along with a bowl of peach jam and looked up at the kitchen ceiling. "Young Lucas stood up for Carrie when Jeremy started pushing her around and hitting her. Jeremy said his father told him it was quite all right to hit or push anyone he wanted. When he tried to hit Carrie, Lucas stepped in and knocked Jeremy to the ground. Ed lost his temper when he heard that and was about to drive one of his fists into my face when I threw the hot coffee in his face."

Constable Kennedy saw no tears, no sobbing, no regrets in the lady's face nor did he hear any crying or whimpering. "He reached his hands out for my neck, Tobias, and that's when I hit him with the frying pan. I'm terribly sorry the man died, but he will never touch me again, never hurt Carrie again."

She walked to the stove and poured them more coffee. "That's the whole story. I don't believe I broke the law in having to protect myself and my children. They will be forced to grow up without a father because of his actions, not mine."

"There will be a hearing before a magistrate, Irene. As you know, many men believe they have a God-given right to hit, spank, or punish their women. I'm not one of them, but I'm not the final authority either. You'll be notified of dates and times. I must insist that you not leave the village."

"What about my children, Tobias? What about them?" She was not able to maintain her stoic demeanor another moment. As she mentioned her children, a flood of tears rolled from her eyes and great sobs echoed off the kitchen walls. She covered her face with her apron and laid her head on the table. "They are the ones he hurt the most and are going to keep being hurt."

"Father O'Reilly and Doctor Winston both believe it's best if the children remain where they are, but that you should visit as often as possible. The Connor family have been your friends for many years."

Oh, that dear woman and those babies. She's got a bit of a row to hoe. What man would look to her thinking all the time, she killed one husband, I'll not be next.

. . .

FRANK AND SABRINA CONNOR HAD A HOMESTEAD CLOSE to the village where, along with cattle and sheep, they raised their children. Isaac was ten and Edith, a childish eight years. Some say she would always be a child and allowed for her short comings. She was a charming little girl who showered love on everyone.

Sabrina Connor was the first to come to Irene Creighton's side after learning of the problem and took the children home with her. "You're right, Constable," Irene said. "Sabrina is a dear friend and I know the children will be safe, well fed, and warm." She refused to break down again in front of Tobias Kennedy, refused to show the least remorse from her actions, but wanted to. She would but not until she was alone.

I should have listened to my father. The man was a rock and I was impetuous to a fault. Look what's come of that. I have my home, I will keep my children, and I'll find a way to keep us fed and warm. The sobs and heartbreak were never seen by anyone after the constable left.

Irene drove the family carriage to the Connor spread to see the children and work out how best to pay them something. Irene was nearing thirty and Sabrina was twenty-five, and the two became best friends almost from their first meeting some three years before. For the most part the children got along, but Jeremy's bullying was not appreciated by young Ike Connor.

"I'm deathly afraid, Sabrina. I will have no income, two children, and an immense and ugly house to maintain. I'll not be able to get you any money for the children. What will I do?"

"We'll have to work this out as we go, Irene. Your children are welcome with us for as long as it takes. Ike and Jeremy will work with Frank and I know Edith and Carrie will get along just fine."

"I'll be putting our home up for sale as soon as all the legalities are done with. Constable Kennedy is sure there'll be no charges following all the investigations. I just don't know what I'll do. I have never been in this position. I'm not a good seamstress, not the best cook around. What am I going to do?"

The ugly truth of the situation was closing in and Irene, like most people who find themselves in her position, wasn't prepared. Still attractive but with two children, living on the frontier but without a means of support, and now with a reputation of having killed her husband, there was little in the world of expectations.

It was later that evening, after having spent the day with her children, that she found herself at her kitchen table, working out her finances. She did the family budgets, even took care of Mr. Creighton's homestead finances, and the open ledger book almost came to life in her eyes.

"Numbers," she almost whispered. "Keeping the books. The only thing Ed Creighton said I was good at. I'll open a bookkeeping service." She rushed into the library that Creighton kept and pulled down three books on accounting law, government contracts, and personal indemnity. "There are lumber companies, freight companies, and warehouse companies that will soon be demanding my services."

There was light in her eyes for the first time in two weeks. She might be able to keep this old house despite its ugliness and was sure to be able to feed her children and keep them warm. *It will be a fight but with my new reputation of being able to fight back, I'll make it in their big old man's world.* There was a smile on her face as she started planning on how to organize the house and create the Irene Creighton Book-Keeping Service.

Tomorrow is Christmas and I'll be with the children. They won't understand but I'm sure I'll get some good discussion with Frank and Sabrina.

CHAPTER 6

"You have to get that mule in the morning, Jacob."
Martha had her arms wrapped around the man's shoulders, snuggled deep in their goose down stuffed mattress, and under wool blankets. The wind had the trees singing, snow drove furious and blinding clouds onto the windows, and the Franklyn fireplace was blazing. The lamp was out and there was romance in her thoughts.

"I know." It might have gone further if she hadn't mentioned the mule. Jacob's mind was back on business. "There's also the question of whether or not I have that hundred acres. I'm going into town first thing and talk with Tobias Kennedy. Thank all the gods of ancient Greece I got that receipt from Creighton before he was killed."

"So sad, for Irene and the children."

"I never did particularly like the gentleman, but his wife seemed to be a nice woman." He chuckled gently remembering how Lucas said that Mrs. Creighton didn't bake the best cookies. "I've heard rumors to the effect that she will open a bookkeeping business. I hope she's better with numbers than she is with cookies."

"That wasn't very nice, Jacob Hoagland." He hugged her tight and related what Luke said about the cookies. "Well, then, all right, but don't be spreading that around," she said. The raging winter storm's rage had them asleep in no time.

"Looks like more than half a foot of snow, Lucas. I want you to make sure we can get to the wood shack and the barn." Jacob and son Luke were shoveling. "I have to go into town and then pick up one last load at Mr. Engle's place. Make sure your mama has plenty of wood for the stove and keep the fire going in the fireplace. Can you do all that?"

"I'm seven years old, Daddy. I'm half a man," he said. He stood as tall as he could, his shoulders squared and his feet slightly spread. He was a big boy, knew it, and was ready to take on the world if need be. "Christmas is almost here. Should I put hay in that empty stall?"

Oh, Luke, you're a sly little feller but I'm not giving in. "I think if St. Nick thinks there should be some, he'll leave it," Jacob said. Just a hint of a smile crossed his face and Lucas frowned, not getting the answer he so much wanted to hear.

Christmas. The word danced in Jacob's head. *So different here on the frontier. I can remember my grandfather talking about when he was just a boy. When the Ohio Valley was the frontier. When the fear of Indian attack was always in one's mind and there wasn't always enough to eat.* Lucas had a shovel five feet long and filled with snow.

"Can't lift it, Daddy."

"Drag it to the side and dump it. That's the way I was taught." Jacob laughed and Lucas giggled as the boy fought it through to the dump. "Good boy."

Food on their frontier must have been different from when I grew up. Lack of food? Not when I was Luke's age. It was family, the entire clan, with long tables filled with roasted ducks and geese, great roasts of venison, and singing. Oh, the singing. From thirty or more adults, and children by the score. He looked at his son and made a vow that Christmas would always mean family to Lucas as well. "Let's see if Mama has some hot chocolate for us, eh? Put in quite a job on that snow, Luke. Good job."

"Good morning, Constable," Jacob said. "Cold one today."

"Morning, Mr. Hoagland. I have a letter here for you. It's from Territorial Judge Wendell in Oregon City." Jacob read the brief note and smiled.

So, we now own another one hundred acres of good bottom land. Engle couldn't make it work but I know we can. So many conflicting stories about old man Creighton, but it looks like he followed through on this one. Jacob folded the note and shoved it in his pocket. *Martha will be pleased.*

"Thank you. Looks like Ed Creighton did the right thing with the Engle property. Is Mrs. Creighton getting along all right? It must be awfully difficult with two children and Christmas, too."

"She has a couple of companies signed up for her bookkeeping business, the children will be coming home in time for Christmas, and the Connors will be glad to see young Jeremy out of their place. That boy is worse than his father, I'm afraid. Has no respect for anything except himself." Constable Kennedy had seen many children raised in the little village and knew, almost instinctively, that he would be dealing with Jeremy Creighton often as the boy grew up.

"Thanks again, Constable and have a Merry Christmas," Jacob said. He patted the pocket where the letter confirming his right to Engle's property was and set off to pick up an old black mule, its saddle and bridal. *Lucas might not get a pinto pony, but he'll get a good working mule that he can ride with dignity.*

So many things to think about when you're driving a small carriage and leading a good mule. What would happen to Martha and Luke if something terrible happened to him? How can he arrange things for such a problem? Who could she turn to? *Granted, Mrs. Creighton brought on her own problems, but they are just as real. Ed Creighton must have been an animal to force a woman to do such a thing. How would Martha react if something dreadful happened to me?*

It was then he turned the question around. *How would I get along without Martha? No, I won't think about such a thing. No.* One can't simply shut off a thought such as that one. It lingered, shadowy in the curtains of his conscious thoughts all the way home.

"THANK YOU, LUKE. THIS IS WONDERFUL." MARTHA HAD her wood bin in the kitchen filled to overflowing and knew the fire in the front room was burning hot. "Your father will be proud, son." They were just a day from Christmas, and she was surprised finding herself even thinking about it.

Jacob's memories of Christmas were so much different than hers. Yes, she remembered, he talked about the wonderful church services and prayers, but it was the joy of family gatherings he remembered. Feasting and singing. Martha's family, while tight and loving, spent untold hours in church services at Christmas. There was no feasting, no singing, few exchanges of gifts.

"I like the way we do Christmas," she mumbled. *That first year when Jacob cut a tree and brought it in the house was quite a surprise. And then helping me put on a feast for seven people or more, and it was just us. Now, I wouldn't have it any other way.*

"Come on, son, let's make some cookies and surprise your father when he gets here."

CHAPTER 7

I rene Creighton was driving her small carriage to the Connor ranch on a cold Christmas Eve morning. She was brimming with anticipation of having her children back home with her. Her cheeks were bright red from the cold and her fingers throbbed for a while and then went numb as she drove the sluggish old mare through some deep drifts on the long ride through rolling hill country.

It just doesn't feel like Christmas. This isn't what I wanted, what the children need. Christmas was always gay, full of prayers of good will and tables full of the earth's bounty. It's my fault, not Ed Creighton's. I should have listened to my father, should have understood his concern. Should have said no.

She stopped her herself almost in mid-thought and wondered. It seemed that every time Creighton took his anger out on her, with fists, with belts, with the most hurtful words, she in turn would blame herself for not listening to her father. *That's just not right. That's like saying I'm to blame and I'm not. Ed Creighton was evil and my only blame is letting it go on as long as it did. Yes, I should have listened to my father. And, no. This is not my fault.*

It felt good, getting that little argument settled. She was able to enjoy the rest of the ride through open land, leading from the timbered riverbanks to open rolling hills soon to be covered in grains and grasses. She breathed the frozen air, blew clouds of steam, along with the mare, and saw the beauty of the landscape.

The house she hated so much had a few touches of the season. Some candles about instead of the oil lamps, some boughs she cut from the fir and pine trees that dotted the property, and a scene of the Bethlehem birth of Christ. "We'll have roast chicken, say prayers to the baby Jesus, and I have just one gift each for the children. Ed Creighton, I'll never forgive you for ruining our family." She surprised herself, speaking right out like that.

I'm a different woman now. Not the fearful little waif who allowed herself to be used, whipped, bruised, and bloodied. No man will ever lay his hands on me or my children again. She turned into the lane leading to the Connor home. *Jeremy will have to learn that his father was not what a man should be. He's young. He'll learn.*

Sabrina Connor hurried down from the porch when Irene drove up. "Let me help you," she said, taking the tie-down rope and attaching it to the post. "Slippery, honey. Be careful," she said, helping Irene out of the carriage. "We'll be thankful for this snow come spring, but not today," she laughed. "Let's get in where it's warm."

"Are the children ready? I want to get back home as soon as possible. Tomorrow's Christmas and I'm not ready."

"Let's talk about that when we get inside," Sabrina

said. The tinkle of laughter was gone as was the smile. Worry replaced the smiles. She hurried ahead and got the door open for them. None of the children were in the gaily decorated front room, but Frank Connor was.

"Hello, Irene," he said. "Come in, come in. You must be frozen. Let's go into the kitchen and have some hot coffee."

"Where are the children?"

"They'll be with us shortly." He smiled and led the way into the kitchen, nicely warmed from the cook stove, and poured coffee for the three of them. "There has been a problem, Irene, and I'm afraid we have to find a solution right away." He did not have a smile on his face and Irene took a quick look at Sabrina only to find her almost crying.

Frank Connor was a large, open man, jovial most of the time. His smile blew darkness into the next county, his ribald humor tended to redden the cheeks of many women. The gregarious man was not himself this bitter cold day.

"I don't understand," she said. "A problem with my children? What kind of problem?" She couldn't help herself. She immediately knew that Jeremy had done something, something terrible. The crush of impending doom was heavy and she almost fell, caught herself, and stood rigid.

"This is most difficult, Irene. Please, sit and sip your coffee while I try to explain." Frank Connor was a big man, towered over his wife, and had large hands, gnarled and calloused from hard work. He pulled a chair back for Irene Creighton, saw to it his wife was seated, and took his seat across from Irene.

"I'm afraid your son Jeremy was taught things young boys shouldn't even know about. As you know, our daughter, Edith, is just a bit slow and can be taken advantage of in children's games. She and your daughter Carrie have become dear friends these last two weeks, but I can't say the same for Jeremy."

"Just what has he done, Frank?" Cold tendrils of fear laced their way toward Irene's heart. *Ed Creighton told Jeremy it was all right to hit girls, but what else did that fiend teach my boy? Oh, my God, what has Jeremy done?* "I'm aware of Ed Creighton's short-comings, Frank. What did that fiend teach my son."

Sabrina reached over and took Irene's hand and squeezed it gently. "I'm afraid Jeremy tried to force himself on little Edith. He said some terrible things about women in general and had Edith's clothes almost off of her before I found them. Edith hasn't stopped crying since. I'm so sorry, Irene."

"He's only ten," Irene said. "How would he —- What would he know —- My God." Irene was crying harder than she did the night she killed Ed Creighton, crying harder than she ever had in her life. Her husband used brute force on her regularly until she put an end to it, and now she finds out her own son is also an animal. "What can I do?" She whimpered the words out ever so slowly, looking first to Frank and then to Sabrina.

"The boy needs some strong supervision, Irene." Frank said. When Sabrina told Frank what had happened the big man had to leave the house, went to the barn and split wood for half an hour before he trusted himself to face the boy. He sat staring down at the table, trying to put what happened and what must be done into words.

"He can't be left alone with a girl or even a weak woman, Irene. He's been taught some ugly things, I'm afraid, and he doesn't understand that they are wrong.

He idolizes his father, still, and it will take a long time for him to understand just how wrong Ed Creighton was."

"You're saying Jeremy has to be sent away somewhere?" She looked at the two, at the table, at her shaking hands. *My son is a molester? Is one because his father told him it was all right to take whatever he wanted?* Her eyes pleaded with Frank, but she also knew that he was right. "What do I do? What can I do? His father even had him believe that I was not allowed to scold or reprimand him."

"The best thing you can do is nothing, Irene. I have already sent for the constable, and he should be arriving shortly. The best thing for you to do is let the constable handle this and not say or do anything."

"He's just a baby," she murmured. "Why?" She laid her head on her arms on the table and cried great sobs, calling his name softly with each one. "Why?" *If only I had listened to my father so many years ago. He knew Ed Creighton was not a good man, knew it from the day they met, but I was blinded. I won't let this ruin the rest of my life. I won't. I will not let this destroy Jeremy, if it hasn't already. Fiend. Creighton was a devil, a fiend.*

"I HAVE NO CHOICE IN THE MATTER, MRS. CREIGHTON." Constable Tobias Kennedy stood at the kitchen table holding Jeremy Creighton by the arm. We'll take good care of the boy, but he must be held until a hearing. I'm sure he'll be sent to Oregon Territory's reformatory for boys if these allegations are true. I'm terribly sorry."

"He's just a boy," Irene cried again. "He isn't a criminal. Just a boy."

"He is both, Mrs. Creighton, but in his favor, it's because he has been taught that what he has done is perfectly all right. He will be taught the correct way of life at the boy's school, if it comes to that. Now, say goodbye quickly and we'll be off. Don't make it worse than it is on yourself, or the boy."

As a lawman, Kennedy was a stalwart for upholding the letter of the law, and as a man, he was known for taking rowdy boys into his home, teaching them the values of family, love, and respect. Knocking heads of those who wouldn't reform or teaching respect to those who wanted to be better people drove the man's life. That and his walking stick.

Irene tried to hug Jeremy but he pulled back from her and Constable Kennedy was astute enough to know he had to get the boy out and away just as soon as possible. "Come now, Jeremy. Time to go," and he tightened his grip on the boy's arm and led him from the house. Jeremy didn't fight back, simply walked out with Kennedy.

Why shouldn't he? After all, what he was doing with the stupid little girl is what his father spent hours telling him it was quite all right. Sure, he'll go with the constable, they'll learn that he didn't do anything wrong. Kennedy could almost read those kinds of thoughts in the boy's face and demeanor. *The lad's but ten. It's for the best that his father will not be with him, ever. He'll be a hard case, and that's for sure.*

Irene stood stock still, eyes wide open but not bright or shiny, her tiny fists knotted so tight the fingers ached, and watched in horror as Jeremy was placed in the cage at the rear of Kennedy's police wagon. "No," she whimpered and knew her knees were giving out. Frank Connor caught her before she hit the floor and carried her to the front room's large divan.

"Cover her, Sabrina, and stay with her. I'll get us all

more coffee." Frank's nerves and bravery had been tested many times as he and Sabrina made their way from St. Louis to this lush Oregon country so many years ago, but this was different, and he felt helpless in the face of Irene's growing problems.

How will she manage all of this? No husband and now a child being charged with a heinous crime? How would Sabrina react? Horror on horror on horror. My God, how would I react? Frank stoked the fire in the kitchen and found the bottle of whiskey he kept in a cupboard. *We all need a little bit of this, I think.*

He brought the bottle, coffee pot, and cups into the living room. Irene was laid out on the divan, covered in a quilted spread. Her eyes were closed, and she was breathing regularly, not gasping or sobbing. "She looks so peaceful," Frank said. "I'll go take care of her horse and carriage, Sabrina. She must stay with us. She can't go home, not yet. Not on Christmas Eve."

Sabrina noticed, and with a slightly hidden smile, watched Frank slip the bottle of whiskey into his coat pocket as he walked out the door. *Strong enough to lift a horse if he wanted to, but a crying and hurting woman turns the man soft. To think I almost said no those many years ago when he asked for my hand. My father knew, though. He knew just what kind of man Frank Connor is.*

CHAPTER 8

J acob Hoagland had one more little problem to solve. "How am I going to get this mule into a stall in the barn without Lucas knowing?" The thrill of being a child and finding that special gift on Christmas morning never left the man. With his father, grandfather, uncles, and aunts always around during holidays, excitement ran high. "It was always the simple gifts that meant so much," he murmured. "This two-dollar mule is more than simple," he chuckled, "but it will mean considerable to that boy."

He was still a mile from the home place, the wind carried its own spears of ice blowing down from the trees, and the answer of how to get that mule home came to him. *If I just drive this wagon in and to the barn he's sure to hear or see me, but if I take the old orchard trail in, he'll never know.*

The orchard road was a game trail at first that led across a creek and through apple trees that had been left to go wild by someone well before the Hoagland family arrived. Jacob trimmed the trees, gave them proper care, and they have produced well enough that there was always cider and hard cider along with plenty of fresh apples to eat and make pies.

It was a rough trail, that is, not maintained, but not the least difficult for horses and mules and Jacob made the run with ease.

From a single-track game trail, use by wagons and buggies over the years turned it into a two track trail that Hoagland's horses had no trouble navigating. As they moved down into a narrow draw and toward the creek, they spooked a magnificent deer and Jacob watched in delight as it pranced its way into deep timber.

"So, looking to eat my apples were you? You would have done nicely in a meat barrel," he mused. The creek crossing was easy as was the ascent on the other side. He had his horses at an easy walk across one meadow, around a hillside, and down into the farmyard and the barn. "So far, so good," Jacob muttered. He had the black mule tucked in its new stall and threw some hay in before un-harnessing his team and putting them up.

He left the barn and was halfway to the house when he saw two buggies tied off in the front of the house. "Well now. Guests on Christmas Eve? Strange." He hurried in through the kitchen door to find Constable Kennedy and another man having coffee with Martha and Lucas.

"Well," Jacob said, "am I late for a meeting?"

Martha laughed. "No, but the constable has some bad news, I'm afraid. This is Doctor Winslow."

"Bad news, Constable? On Christmas Eve?" Jacob poured coffee and sat down. "Seems to be going around these days. Doctor? I don't believe we've met."

"Only because you're healthy, young man. My pleasure," he said, offering his hand. Kennedy got right to the point of the visit.

"You're familiar with what happened with the Ed Creighton family, but I'm afraid it has gotten worse for the woman." Kennedy looked over to Doctor Winslow for help.

"It's been charged by Frank Connor that the Creighton boy attempted to sexually attack their daughter Edith. He's in custody now." Winslow said.

"Oh, my God. That's terrible," Jacob said. He looked to Martha and shook his head. She offered a sad smile and dropped her gaze to the table. "Why are you bringing this news to us?" Jacob looked again at Martha then Lucas. "Luke, I wonder if maybe you should find somewhere else to be right now."

"No, Mr. Hoagland, I think he needs to hear this. It seems that young Jeremy Creighton has a great dislike for Lucas," Doctor Winslow said. "Jeremy has been taking advantage of his sister for some time, but Lucas here put a stop to it a few weeks ago."

"I did," Luke said. He looked at his father. "Remember? When we were in the village to see Mr. Creighton."

"I remember, son, but I still don't understand how that would have anything to do with Jeremy attempting something that horrible on Connor's daughter." Jacob was getting frustrated. He still had Christmas, Luke's mule, surprises on his mind, not something as gross as a little boy attacking a girl. "Let's put it all on the table, shall we? Remember, gentlemen, it's Christmas Eve and plans have been made. This is absurd, gentlemen. Lucas is seven years old. How could he have anything to do with this?"

"No, Jacob, you may have misunderstood what we're saying." Winslow stood up and walked around the table to where Lucas was sitting, next to his mother. "I've spent the last few hours talking with Jeremy and it appears that his father taught him some exceedingly unfavorable ways of associating with girls and women. Is that true, Lucas?" Doctor Winslow asked. "Did the boy ever say anything about how to treat a girl or a woman?"

"That's why I knocked him down," Lucas said. "He said his father insisted that it was all right to do anything with a girl or woman, that they were there to serve men."

Martha gasped. "Lucas," she said. "Jacob. How could he do that? My heavens."

"It's all right, Martha," Jacob said. "Luke and I have had a couple of long talks about this, eh son? Luca knew immediately that what Jeremy was saying was wrong. What are you here for, exactly, Doctor? Constable? You seem to be unwilling to say what's on your mind."

"What Lucas just said, Mr. Hoagland. We needed to hear Lucas say that. I didn't believe Jeremy, thought he was lying, but I was wrong. You have a fine, boy, Hoagland. Fine indeed." Doctor Winslow stood up to leave. "Creighton had no use for women, and he passed his hatred on to his son."

"I assume there will be hearings of some kind? I do not want Lucas involved in any way," Jacob said.

Yes, there will be," Constable Kennedy said. "Lucas has knowledge of the boy and why he acts the way he does, but he is too young to testify. We will ask that he make written statements that can be entered into the record."

"I will be present at any discussions that will be held with Lucas," Jacob said. "Our boy has been raised as a gentleman, sir, and always shows respect for girls and women, his elders, and his parents. I'll not allow any railroading by men who think they have the right. I won't."

"He'll be treated with the utmost care and respect, Mr. Hoagland," Doctor Winslow said. "And you and your wife will be more than welcome at any discussions we hold with Lucas."

Jacob didn't like the idea of Lucas being involved in this, wasn't going to let grown men browbeat his boy into saying something that would get someone in a lot of trouble. *Jeremy Creighton may have done the things he's accused of, but Lucas wasn't involved at all and these people better understand that.* "I'll hold you to that, Doctor." He reached out and pulled Lucas to him and hugged him tight. "The Hoagland name will not be sullied by any of this."

"What about Mrs. Creighton?" Martha asked. "She has been through, well, I can't say what I want to say. What will come of this?"

"I'm afraid the boy will be sent to a reformatory, maybe for a long time." Constable Kennedy said.

"And Mrs. Creighton is just left adrift? That poor woman." Martha looked at Jacob, tears welling in her eyes. "She has a daughter, too. My God, Jacob, this isn't right."

"No, it isn't but I'm not sure there's anything we can do." Jacob stood behind her and gently rubbed her shoulders, could feel the tension in her, and hoped the Creighton problems wouldn't come to nest in the Hoagland farm.

"We'll be leaving now. Thank you, Lucas. You've been a big help," Constable Kennedy said. "Merry Christmas to you."

Jacob ushered the two out and came back to the kitchen quickly. "Strange," he muttered. "There's something more than hearing Lucas tell them what Jeremy might have said."

"There is," Martha said. "I don't think you picked up on it. The doctor said that Jeremy may have been doing to his sister what he is charged with, what he attempted to do to the Connor girl." Martha was still crying as she said it, and Lucas went to her side.

"He's a mean bully, Mama, and he says his father told him he can do to any girl or woman whatever he wants. That it's a man's right."

"Well, son," Jacob said, "we know it isn't and we know it's our responsibility to not let it happen, don't we?"

"Yes, we do," Lucas said. He had his arms around his mother, and she ran her fingers through his long blondish hair. "Nobody will ever hurt you, Mama."

Martha continued crying softly, squeezed her boy tight and looked at Jacob. "We must find a way to help that woman, Jacob. No husband, a son in custody, and a daughter who may have been molested. We can't let this just slip away."

"She's a very strong woman, Martha. She will need help, but I think she's capable of far more than you might believe. We'll keep our eyes and ears open for opportunities to help." Jacob knew in his heart that there would be far more than what he indicated. Martha was going to get them involved. *Martha is a good woman and isn't going to let this pass.*

CHRISTMAS EVE SUPPER WAS A QUIET AFFAIR. LUKE HAD thoughts of finding a pinto pony in the stall the next morning, knew he would be riding the high-stepping courser through knee deep snow, laughing and singing. Jacob had thoughts of all the new ground that would need to be plowed, planted, and harvested in the coming year, and Martha only had thoughts of knowing what a wonderful family she had. One that would see a new face at the table in the coming year.

"Amazing how things can change so fast, isn't it?" Martha said as they slipped under a heavy quilt. "Just weeks ago, you were afraid the world was against you and now you're the proud owner of another hundred acres of good land that will fight you."

Jacob laughed and wrapped his arms around her. "You have a way with words, Mrs. Hoagland. Zeb Engle's land is going to be good for us, our son is growing up a gentleman, and I will see to it that you will never be hungry, cold, or hurt."

"I don't want to think just how hard it must be for Irene Creighton right now. No husband, son in detention, and Christmas Eve. Is there anything we can do? Anything?"

"I don't know," Jacob said. "She has her bookkeeping business so they will eat and be warm. She'll be a good mother to the girl. It may be that she won't need anyone's help."

"She'll need a friend, Jacob. She won't have a big warm guy to snuggle up to at night, to depend on for wood for the fire and kind words when she's hurt. No, she needs a friend more than anything right now."

"Sounds to me like a plan is being made, my lady." The response was more hugs, nibbles on the ear, and a delightful Christmas present, just a few hours early.

Christmas morning found another ten inches of snow on the ground, drifted about by strong winds. It was icy when Lucas ran down the stairs and out the kitchen door. He floundered his way through the drifts to the barn and stood in amazement when he found a tall, very black mule looking at him for breakfast.

"Ho! Hello black mule. You're not a pinto and you're

not a pony either. You're a big mule and I think you're going to be my best friend." Excitement lit the boy's eyes and drove him to almost dancing about the barn. "A big black mule," he said over and over. He found the grain bucket and offered it through the fence. "You need a name, buddy. Yes! Buddy. That's your name. Hello, Buddy, I'm Luke Hoagland and we're gonna be buddies."

He was talking millions of miles an hour and didn't hear Jacob and Martha walk in behind him. Jacob had his arms around Martha, watching the little play unfold, not saying a word. It was Buddy the mule who alerted Lucas to company.

"Mama, Dad, look, look," he was shouting with happiness, dancing, jumping. "My pinto pony is a black mule named Buddy. Look."

"He's big and strong, son. Don't ever forget that. He's yours to ride, to help with farm work, and to care for. You will have to feed him and clean up after him. You know that, right?"

"Oh, yes, Dad. Oh, yes. I know that," Lucas said. "Thank you, Mama, Dad. this is the best Christmas I've ever had."

CHAPTER 9

T he view through the window, iced solid, was simply a gray mat of iced glass. Irene Creighton wiped away a patch of ice and looked out on a scene of fresh snow covering everything. "So clean and always so quiet after a new snow." She tried to be quiet getting the Franklyn stove lit but woke Carrie up when she hit the striker.

The girl was wrapped tight in her blankets and fought hard to get untangled. "Merry Christmas, sweetheart," she whispered. It only took minutes for the stove to warm the bedroom and Irene slipped downstairs to light the kitchen stove, and finally, the front room's fireplace. *"Glad I brought the wood in last night. One more thing to remember now that it's just me and Carrie. So easy to think that. Just me and Carrie. It was cruel the way Doctor Simpson told me of Jeremy's behavior. Cruel. I'll not forgive that man the way he treated Carrie, as if she had something to do with it. I'll not have another man living in this house.*

She had fought it, but the anger just kept coming, just kept building. Irene Creighton had never been an angry person and didn't like what this new feeling brought. *I will be angry at Ed Creighton for a long time, but I have no reason to be angry at those around me. All men are not like Mr. Creighton, but even so, I'll not be getting friendly with any man for a long time.*

Breakfast was simple, a bowl of boiled oats laced with honey, coffee for Irene, milk for Carrie, and they walked into the front room of the now warm house. "It isn't much of a Christmas, I'm afraid, my precious little girl." She handed a small package, gaily wrapped at least, to the girl. "Your grandmother made this and gave it to me when I was a little girl."

Carrie undid the wrapping and squealed with joy finding a stuffed doll, all dressed in taffeta, bows, and ribbon. "Oh, Mama, she's beautiful. Did you give her a name?"

Memories of that Christmas so long ago came in waves, flooding Irene. "Yes," she murmured. "We lived in a small cabin deep in the woods, back then. I called her Maggie."

"Maggie?"

"As in the magpie bird." Irene chuckled, thinking about it. "There was no real reason. Just Maggie. Your grandfather operated a mill and lumber business, hunted for much of our food, and fought off the Indian attacks that seemed to come so often. It was fearful times but joyous and warm, too. That little doll got lots of loving."

"I'll always love her," Carries said. She held the doll close, and Irene could see tears in the child's eyes. "Will I ever get to meet Grandma and Grandpa? You've told me stories. They seem very nice." Carrie was born on the long journey from St. Louis to the Willamette Valley in Oregon Territory and never knew the Ohio Valley of the 1840s, never met any of her relations. "I love them even if I've never met them."

"You'll always have those memories, Carrie. It's the ones we're building now that I fear. We can't let them rot in fear and pain, have to build them into golden memories, let our wildest dreams become reality."

"How, Mama?"

"Today is Christmas, Carrie. Let's start with today and every day we'll do something that we will want to remember down through the years. What should we do today that we will want to remember?"

"Can we go for a walk by the river? It's the prettiest river I've ever seen. So many ducks and geese. Can we?"

"Well bundle up in coats and robes and walk along the river. Maybe even sing a little song," Irene said. It had been some time that her eyes sparkled as they did that morning. *Walking along our peaceful river, just me and Carrie. Yes.* She closed her eyes and could almost see the little creek that ran by their cabin back in the Ohio Valley. It was peaceful most of the time. Indian attacks generally came from the stream, though, and no one walked its banks alone.

Even the frightful Indian attacks weren't as terrible as what's happening right now. How can I protect Carrie when I'm not sure I can even protect myself?

FRANK CONNOR WAS UP WITH THE SUN ON CHRISTMAS morning, saw the fresh snow through the upstairs window and smiled. "Spring water," he murmured. He stirred the banked coals, added some kindling, and had a good blaze crackling and popping in minutes. *Best thing I ever thought of, building a rock fireplace in the bedroom.* The flue connected to the main chimney from downstairs and allowed for larger, warmer fires in the bedroom.

He decided to let his wife, Sabrina sleep in on this

special holiday and headed downstairs to get the kitchen fires lit. "Well now," Frank said. "Two little gremlins up and about, eh? Merry Christmas, children. Ike, did you fill the wood boxes last night?" He was surprised to find the cook stove fire popping away. Even a pot of coffee was ready to brew.

"Yes, sir, Papa, and Edith helped me. I lit the fire, too." Isaac, called Ike from the moment of his birth, was ten-years-old and his sister, Edith, was eight. "Edie ground the beans and did a good job."

Edith was 'slow', as children with learning problems were described, but was as loving a daughter as Frank Connor could wish for. "That's fine. Thank you, Edie. Let's the three of us surprise your mama and get the house warm and breakfast ready to serve before we wake her up."

Edie danced around, laughing, and Ike made sure there was wood in the stove. "When do we get to open our presents, Papa?"

"We'll have our breakfast, say some prayers to the baby Jesus, and then sit around the tree, son. Looks like we got a good snow last night. Maybe we can climb the orchard hill and sled back down a few times."

"Yes," Ike said. "Yes."

Ike lit the fireplace in the front room while Frank and Edie started breakfast. "Hot cakes, some smoked side meat, and scrambled eggs. That good with you, Edie?"

"I'll go get Mama up," she said.

Frank watched her run up the stairs, laughing loudly, and wondered just how much damage the Creighton boy had inflicted on the child. How much on Sabrina? "What a foul man to teach his boy such terrible things. Another few minutes and things would have been far worse." He was still muttering when Ike came in from the front room and Sabrina and Edie came down the stairs.

"I have the most wonderful family on the frontier," Frank said. "Merry Christmas to you all. Let's have breakfast and check under the tree, eh? Have we had a late-night visitor?" The children wanted to run and see but knew breakfast came first. "I just wonder what might be there?" Frank continued to tease.

"I hope I get my tools," Ike said. "I built the forge, Papa, "but I can't build a bellows like you have. I want a bellows and some hammers and tongs."

"You amaze me, Ike," Sabrina said. "I would never think that you would like that kind of hard work. Heavy iron, heavy hammers, hot fire."

"I'm going to make some new hinges for the barn doors, Mama. You just wait. All fancy iron work. Like at the courthouse."

"Amazing," is all Sabrina could say.

"He's taught himself, Sabrina. He is amazing. I think he'll probably work with Ben Thorndyke next year. It's a fine craft and always there is a need for a good blacksmith."

Such a difference, Sabrina thought, looking around the table. *Poor, dear, Irene Creighton has no family left. It's just her and Carrie and some terrible memories. What will happen to that horrid boy? Well, I hope it's as horrible for him as it has to have been for Edie. Horrible.*

The gifts were opened, a song or two sung, and Frank was ready to go sledding. "I'd rather not," Sabrina said. You all go and have as much fun as you can."

"Why, Sabrina. You've always loved sledding."

"I can't get Irene Creighton out of my mind, Frank. Just she and Carrie. Horrible memories. Terrible Christmas. What will become of them?"

"She's a strong woman, Sab. You've said that yourself, many times."

"She needs a friend, Frank. Someone other than a child to talk to."

"You have someone in mind, do you?" He chuckled ushering the children out the door.

The man knows me too well, Sabrina thought. *Maybe I'll take a little buggy ride tomorrow and pay my respects.*

MID-MORNING CHRISTMAS MEAL AT THE HOAGLAND FARM was quiet, filled with warmth and thoughts of the coming year. "Buddy and I can help with the plowing and clearing, can't we, Dad?"

"Yes, son, I think you can. If these snows keep up, we won't have water problems. What we do have, though, is another one hundred acres to work. Old Engle wasn't very good at laying out his plots. We'll be making some changes."

Hoagland had a satisfied look on his craggy face as he smiled at Lucas and Martha. *My boy isn't old enough or big enough to run a plow or drag roots from the ground, but he'd give it his all if he had to. I'm one lucky man.* Those thoughts of 'what might happen' that he had driving the equipment and mule back from Engle's place tried to invade his thoughts. *No, I won't think about that on this wonderful morning. What I will think about is just what a fine family I have.*

"If we're going to have an expanded kitchen garden, like you talked about, Jacob, vegetables for sale in town, I'll need Lucas's help, too. The coming baby will slow me down some, big boy." She almost giggled and rubbed her not yet expanding tummy.

"You're going to be eight-years-old this spring, young

man, and I'm afraid I'm going to have to ask you to grow up fast. It's a good thing you're big and strong, but you'll be working like you're twelve, I'm afraid." He tried to smile but it didn't happen. The boy's too young to be asked to do these things, kept running though his mind.

Not enough money to hire anyone and now I'm going to work my boy too hard. Shouldn't have taken on Engle's property. Selfish, that's what I am. Want more than I can work just to have it. Then he remembered the stories his father and grandfather told of the earlier days in the Ohio Valley, how they worked right alongside the older men building the homes, stockades, even fight off Indian attacks.

My grandfather wasn't but seven when he worked a team of mules hauling logs for the stockade. He always said it made him the man he was. I worked alongside my father, too. No, it isn't selfish, it's family.

"We have time to work out the details. Let's hitch up the mules and take a ride down along the river. It should be beautiful this morning, with all the fresh snow."

"Oh, I've forgotten about that," Martha said. It seemed like the entire village of Brookside turned out on Christmas morning to promenade along the river and through the town. "Fresh snow will make it even more beautiful," she said.

"I'll saddle up Buddy and ride with you," Lucas cried out. His eyes sparkled and his smile was ear to ear.

"No, son, riding with a hundred other buggies, wagons, and outriders wouldn't be safe for your first ride on your new mule. Best do that in the pastures where no one might get hurt. We'll ride in our wagon and say Merry Christmas to all."

CHAPTER 10

B ells were ringing from the two churches in the village and those that attended services were moving toward them. Children were out showing off their new toys, sleds, dolls, and clothing, while adults were doing their best to catch their breath. Many families, it seemed, had the same idea as Irene Creighton and Jacob Hoagland.

"My goodness," Irene said as the two walked up to the level walkway along the river's levee. There were many families on the walkway and many more in buggies and wagons along the tree lined roadway. "Looks like it's going to be a busy time out here."

People with new winter coats, jackets, and capes were strutting their stuff, men in new beaver hats and buffalo long coats, women in furs from fox, sable, wolf, bear, and buffalo rode in buggies and wagons coated in fall and winter mud. Children ran everywhere, some singing, some just yelling in pure happiness.

"It's wonderful, Mama," Carrie said. She was laughing, almost dancing, watching the parade of people.

I wonder if this is a tradition in our village? Irene

thought as she watched the happy throng. *Ed Creighton would never take part in something as joyous as this. Frivolous, he'd say. Have we missed this all these years?* "I'm so glad we came down here, Carrie. Keep Maggie warm and we'll enjoy all this for another hour." The little girl squealed and hugged her new doll close.

BEN THORNDYKE STOMPED AROUND THE BIG KITCHEN IN his two-story home trying to get people moving. "Snow will melt to mud by the time you're ready to enjoy this day," he growled. His wife Beverly chuckled and did a little skip, which brought a laugh from the large man. "All right, now, have your fun but we really do need to get moving."

Thorndyke owned the largest company in the village, selling farm implements and heavy machinery used in the lumber mills. He had two forges working at all times, building plows, rakes, discs and wheels. Had two men working in the leather shop building harness, head stalls, saddles, and reins. His son, Peter, was twelve and worked in every department of the business. Thorndyke told him, "If you're going to eventually run this place, you better know how to do each and every job that's done."

Thorndyke stood a solid six feet tall and carried considerable weight that was mostly muscle. The gregarious man got his start in business felling timber in Pennsylvania, but it was during the long ride to Oregon Territory that he learned the art of buying and selling. He was a born trader and, as some have said, could sell a pint of rum to a teetotaler.

The boy didn't much care for starting out as the swamper, the boy who cleaned up every night after closing, but Thorndyke saw to it that Peter was the best swamper the company ever had. His other son, Gerald, was born as a cripple, one leg much shorter than the other, and not very strong either. Thorndyke had special shoes built for the boy in his harness shop. High thick sole and heel on one shoe and his feet hit the floor evenly. The man fashioned extraordinary crutches, engraved and inlaid with silver, to help him along.

The boy gained weight and strength but was also a reader, as was his mother. Gerald was fascinated by books about the oceans and more than once told his mother he was going to run away to sea.

The boys were catered to on the one hand but were made to carry their fair share of the load as well. Spoiled? Possibly, but in such a manner as they understood their end of the bargain, knew responsibility. Their father never shirked a job and they learned fast that they shouldn't, either.

"Team is harnessed, Father," Peter said. He held the front door for the family. "You and mother sit in the back and Gerald and I will drive you in style." Ben Thorndyke gave a hearty laugh and escorted Beverly to the carriage.

"Looks like the whole town is along the river," Thorndyke said. "Good. All this fresh snow means a good year for the farms, and plenty of water also means the mills will be working at capacity. It'll be a fine year for the Thorndyke's of Oregon Territory, my dear."

"You'll find any excuse to give a little speech, won't you, Ben?" Beverly chortled, pinching the big man in the ribs. "Ah, I love the smell of winter. Look at all the people." Peter was an excellent coach driver and maneuvered the carriage into a long line of buggies, wagons, carriages, and individual riders.

As they rode along the river, they waved at and got

waved to by most of the town. "Look, Ben," Beverly said, "That's the Creighton woman and her daughter. She killed her husband, you know."

"Man had it coming, Beverly. I threatened to kill him myself, more than once." She looked at him, caught the sly smile, and chuckled. He continued as if all he had said was maybe he'd like more coffee. "Peter, slow to a stop," Thorndyke said. He waved at Irene Creighton to come to the carriage. "Good Christmas to you, Mrs. Creighton. Hello Carrie."

"Good Christmas to you and your family," Irene said. "Such a beautiful morning and so many people."

"It's a tradition, Ma'am, but I don't believe Creighton ever took part." He saw her face cloud and cursed himself for bringing the man's name up. "Sam Hollister tells me you work wonders with numbers."

"I've opened a bookkeeping business, sir, and Mr. Hollister is my first client."

"Well, Ma'am, I'd like to be your second," Thorndyke said. "I apologize for my previous mention."

Irene smiled at the big man and nodded. "I'm afraid you might have to settle for being my fourth client, sir, but I'm fully prepared to take on your business. You for sure would be my biggest client."

"Splendid. Come to my office in the morning and we'll get things started." They shook hands and he nodded to Peter to continue their voyage. Irene stood silent as the carriage moved back into traffic.

"That man is a true gentleman, Carrie, something your father knew nothing about." She had a wonderful smile on her face, red from the cold and a bit of a rush from the conversation. As the two got back onto the pathway, Irene let her mind have some fun, too. *A little Christmas morning stroll along the river and I just became*

58

financially independent, my daughter will not do without because of me, and that horrible old house will get a big make over. If only Jeremy had not done such horrible things because of Ed Creighton. He'll not enjoy the life Carrie and I will and it's Creighton's fault.

THE FIVE-MILE WAGON RIDE INTO TOWN FOR A PROMENADE along the river was filled with Hoagland family singing and the occasional braying of a team of mules. "They sing as well as you, dear husband," Martha laughed. The brilliant sun filled the countryside with glistening crystals and intense colors, while the icy wind made everyone's cheeks bright red.

"Looks like the whole town turned out," Jacob said. He moved the old farm wagon into the line of participants, waving to friends and smiling at all. "I feel as young as Lucas," he said. "So many people, so much joy. I love this."

"Isn't that Ben Thorndyke's carriage?" Martha said, pointing at the stately machine.

"Hello, Hoagland," Thorndyke yelled out. "I tried to file on the Engle's pace and found you beat me out. Good land, my friend. Good land. And, a good Christmas to you and your family."

"And to you and yours, Ben. I'll be in to see you about a few things before spring." They waved as they passed. Lucas hollered out to Peter that he got a mule for Christmas and the boy smiled back.

"I like him," Lucas said. "He knows how to sew leather. Did you know that, Dad?"

"Look, Jacob, there's Mrs. Creighton and Carrie. Oh, please stop so we can say hello." Martha waved to Irene as Jacob pulled the wagon to the side and stopped. "Oh,

Irene, I'm so glad we get to say hello. Will you and Carrie ride with us?"

"It's been some time since we've talked," Irene said. "Yes, I think we'd like that very much." It wasn't until after they were settled that Irene saw the looks that passed between Lucas and her daughter.

"This is the boy who bopped Jeremy when he hit me, Mama. He wouldn't let Jeremy try to hit me again, either. But he doesn't like your cookies."

Lucas blushed, Jacob chuckled, and Martha started to say something. Irene just laughed. "I remember. They didn't turn out very well. If you come visit again, Lucas, I'll have a better batch for you."

"Is there anything that Jacob and I can do, Irene? It must be awfully difficult for you."

I never got to know any of the people in this little village. Irene couldn't hide the smile from the invitation. *I never knew how kind and generous so many are. Ed Creighton was a social boor, hated everyone. Mr. Thorndyke, right out of the blue wants my services, and Mrs. Hoagland asks what I might need. I have missed so much being married to Creighton.*

Her mind drifted for a few seconds, remembering the small villages where she grew up. Tight knit families that would open their hearts and hearths to anyone who needed help. *If they'll let me, I'll become a member of this small community. Carrie and I will.* She realized Martha asked a question and she hadn't responded.

"My new business seems to have found its niche, Martha, and Carrie and I are going to be fine. I'm afraid for Jeremy," she said. Tears welled and she dabbed with a hanky. "He's just a boy, still a baby, and they're treating him like a criminal."

"I'm afraid Ed taught him to be a criminal, Mrs.

Creighton," Jacob said. "It's you and Carrie that will have to work through the mess that man created."

"I'll never simply write the boy off," Irene said. "He's my son, I love him dearly and at the same time know the horrible things he's done. Can he be saved? Only time will tell us that."

They made another circle of the town and dropped Irene and Carrie off in front of their home. "Will you come to supper one night soon?" Martha asked.

"We'll look for an invitation," Irene said. The smile was genuine. "By the way, I'm now the bookkeeper for Ben Thorndyke." She walked and Carrie almost skipped and danced up the pathway to their home.

"They'll be fine, Martha," Jacob said. "It will certainly be a burden, having the whole village know you killed your husband, but she's an intelligent and strong woman. Little Carrie might face problems from some of the children."

"Jeremy doesn't even understand that what he did or tried to do, was wrong. He'll carry that cross for the rest of his life, Jacob." Martha looked over at Lucas. *Almost the same age and worlds apart. My God, Jeremy is considered a criminal and now has no family either.*

CHAPTER 11

I rene Creighton was slightly early for the meeting with Ben Thorndyke and young Gerald took the opportunity to show her around. "Is your daughter not with you?" The boy had an engaging smile splashed across his face that Irene liked.

He's a miniature of his father, she thought. *Wide open to the world, friendly, and gracious. I think I'll enjoy being around these people.* "No, Gerald, this is business. She has some fine reading at home, and she'll be doing her numbers as well."

"I like to read," Gerald said. "Numbers frustrate me, but I can read for hours. Does she have many books?"

"I brought some when we came across," Irene said, "and I have standing orders with a Boston seller for shipments." *This boy is ten and I feel as if I'm chatting with an adult. Carrie is like that.*

"I do, too," Gerald said. It was a simple statement that said so much about the boy. The son of the most successful businessman in the area yet completely unassuming. Gerald was ten and his world was considerably smaller than most boys of his age because of his bad leg.

The deformity didn't slow his mind a bit. "Maybe Carrie and I could do some trading."

"Certainly, something to think about, young man. Ah, here's your father. To work I must go," she laughed, standing to greet Thorndyke.

"Let's start our day with some coffee in my office, shall we? Gerald, can you see to that, please?" He led the way from the front of the spacious reception area to a set of double doors, which he threw open.

"Oh, my," Irene said. They were in a factory, not an office with oak panels and maple desks. A steam engine at the far end drove seven or eight different work areas by way of gears and belts. Men with hammers were pounding red hot sheets of steel while others were using machines to bend steel into intricate forms. The noise was beyond words, she thought, looking at the big man. Her eyes were filled with questions.

"Come along," he said. He had a wonderfully childish smile on his face, as a boy about to pull a prank might have. As they passed each workstation Ben had small conversations with those attending the machines and it was a full twenty minutes before they reached the far end of the building. The steam engine made ghastly noises, Irene was sure it would explode at any second, and Ben led them out the back door of the large building.

The sunshine, a fresh breeze, and quiet flooded her senses as she followed Ben Thorndyke across open land behind the great factory building. "There is my office," he said, pointing at a grove of huge Oregon fir trees surrounding a small, just one room, log cabin. They walked into an eloquent setting. Inlaid parqueted floor-ing, walls of cedar, windows covered in curtains made from various parts of trees and ferns, and a wonderful fireplace featuring field stones from the very ground on which the cabin stood.

"Not quite what you expected, eh?" Thorndyke motioned for her to take a chair in front of the fireplace, and he took the other. "When one lives and works in a setting as magnificent as Oregon, one must be fully involved in what it offers. There is nothing more eloquent than the timber and farm country of Oregon Territory."

Irene was enthralled, speechless, overwhelmed with this tidy little log cabin/office of Ben Thorndyke's. Thorndyke had a table between the two comfortable chairs filled with files and binders.

"Our work," he said. Beverly Thorndyke and Gerald came in, one with a coffee pot, cups and saucers, and the other with small plates of pastry. "Now, we can get started," he said. Beverly kissed him on the cheek, shook hands with Irene, and she and Gerald slipped out as quietly as they came.

She and Thorndyke spent the next four hours going over his many businesses in detail. The retail store, the factories, and distribution. Each had its own set of accounts. "We always need to keep them separated," Thorndyke said. "Can't let those varmints who make harnesses get any of the proceeds from the farm imple-ment factories." There was a hearty chuckle, and it took a second for Irene to join him. After all, both businesses were his anyway.

A contract was written that both agreed to, money matters were discussed and agreed to, and Irene was ready to head back to home, just three short blocks away. "I believe we have accomplished something I've needed for some time, Mrs. Creighton. On your next visit, Gerald will escort you to your own office, not quite like this, you understand." He laughed right out. But it will be warm and comfortable. Please, too, while I'm thinking about it, feel free to bring Carrie with you. She shouldn't be left alone."

This man is aware of how much he needs accounting help and at the same time how much I will need help with Carrie. I thought our meeting would be the first of many before I could even start. So easy to work out all the details because he needs help. She couldn't control the smile as they shook hands and saw considerable warmth in Thorndyke's return smile.

"During your busiest times I'll be here three days a week, sir," she said, "and at others, I think everything can be handled with two days work." She'd found a mish-mash of bookwork that would take her some time to re-arrange. "I'll take the next several days creating a proper set of books for us to work from."

"I've wanted that for a long time," Thorndyke said. He shook his large head and gave her an almost child-like grin. "I just didn't know how to do it." He laughed and shook his head again. "I can sell anything. My people can build anything, but what you're talking about? I know not a shred of what you're talking about. I'll have those ledgers you need made available on the next shipment coming in from Oregon City. Two weeks, maybe."

That's wonderful," she said. It was a nice walk in the cold of a winter afternoon and Irene wanted to shout it out to the world. *We're going to be just fine.* She stopped at the bakery on the way home for small sweet cakes for her and Carrie to enjoy before supper.

The next several days were a blur of activity, arranging proper ledgers for the various businesses and finding time to shop for victuals. She brought Carrie to the Thorndyke compound each day along with a couple of books, paper and pencils, and Carrie's favorite doll. Gerald would pop in from time to time and he and Carrie would read.

Irene sat at the kitchen table nursing a last cup of hot coffee, almost asleep, but with a smile. *From a few days before Christmas to this. From a sure beating from Ed Creighton to losing Jeremy, to being bookkeeper for Thorndyke. Life has strange ways of playing with us mortals.*

CHAPTER 12

Constable Kennedy left his office following a midday meeting with Territorial Judge Anthony Petrini. A scowl that could be seen half a block away covered his ruddy face as he plowed through drifts of icy snow. *This will not have a happy ending.*

"I tell you, Claude, the man has no business sitting in that chair. He's not had a minute's time reading the law."

"I agree, but he holds the office. I'll draw up the letter to the governor." Claude Atkins was the county attorney and prosecutor of the Jeremy Creighton case.

Territorial Judge Petrini, about sixty, thin as a rail, and tall to boot, saw children as angels, felt most women needed a good thrashing often, and the few friends he had were hard drinkers. There were some who believed he might have been married but it was well in his past. Petrini came west with the American Fur Company and was involved in some of the disputes with the larger Hudson Bay Company. Not as a club wielding battle participant, but as a negotiator, thus being named Territorial Judge without papers, so to speak.

Kennedy fought is way to the swept and shoveled pathway to the Creighton home and banged on the door. "I'm terribly sorry to barge in like this," Kennedy said. "Something has happened that you need to know, I'm afraid," he said when Irene came to the door. She saw a forlorn, beaten man, not the tall, strong constable who had looked after her best interests.

"Please, come in, Constable. My heavens. Can I get you a cup of coffee?"

"Yes, and with a spot of rum, if its available." He followed her into the kitchen and sat down at the table. "Judge Petrini has just changed the orders that were handed down by the county attorney."

"Oh, my. In what way?" Irene asked. County Attorney Claude Atkins was to lead the prosecution of Jeremy Creighton and planned to ask that the young boy be remanded to a farm for disreputable boys, located near Oregon City. His crimes had been discussed on every street corner, farmyard, and work room in the village for weeks. "I don't like the look on your face."

There were few boys known to have ever left what was called the Boys' Farm. Those that did were generally locked up in adult prisons soon after their release. "The Boy's Farm was not my first hope," Irene said, "but surely they wouldn't send a boy, so young, to a men's facility. What did Judge Petrini say?"

"He wants to lower the charges to a simple misde-meanor and have the boy work off a small sentence cleaning the courthouse. He doesn't consider what Jeremy did as a serious crime. Just a young boy's playing. He wants to release the boy back to your custody."

Irene stood stock still at the comment, her hands on her hips, rage slowly building. "My God, no," she said. Fear flushed her face and she found her hands trembling at the thought of Jeremy being in close proximity to Carrie. She found a chair and sat down, holding her head in her hands. The crying came quickly.

"He's blaming me, isn't he. He's saying I was wrong in killing Ed Creighton and this is how he will punish me. My son learned to be a brute, taught to do things only evil men did, and this judge wants me to have him live in this house? I'll not have it."

"That might be a little strong, but you're far more right than wrong," Kennedy said. "I'm taking a message to the Territorial Governor in the morning. Atkins and I, along with others, including Ben Thorndyke, are asking the governor to intervene. Nothing will be done before he makes a decision."

"Thank you, Constable. You're a good man. Thank you. What can I do?" *I won't have Jeremy living in this house. I won't. I won't let him get within ten feet of Carrie. No, no.* She and Constable Kennedy sat at the table, quietly, for several more minutes. No one could hear the rage in Irene's head.

What kind of man is this Judge Petrini to even consider sending Jeremy back to this home? This home where he constantly abused his sister, where he learned horrible things from his father? What kind of man would do that?

"Let me get you another coffee, Constable. Another spot of rum?" She put an earthen jug on the table when she brought the coffee pot over. "This and two others were gifts to Creighton for getting someone some land."

"Really?" Kennedy's eyes opened up a bit as he nudged the cork out and enjoyed the delicious aroma of Virginia rum. He knitted his brows before asking if there might have been other gifts coming to Creighton for performing his land office duties.

"Oh, yes. To him, not to me or the children. Knives,

guns, two mules once that he sold immediately. Why do you ask?"

"It's against territorial law for the land manager to accept gifts from those attempting to acquire land. It's called bribery, Mrs. Creighton. Of course, it's all moot now, but Creighton could very well have faced prison time for accepting those bribes."

"As I recall, Constable, he solicited them," she said. *Now I find out I was married to a criminal and I might be forced to allow my criminal son to live in this house? No.* "They can't force me to take Jeremy back into our home, can they?"

"I'm afraid so. He is, after all, your son. What he attempted to do is criminal, Mrs. Creighton, but the judge is the judge. Only the governor can change that." They had more coffee, the constable had more rum, and Kennedy left an hour or so later. Irene didn't say anything to Carrie during their supper and the two went to bed rather early.

It was a night filled with terrible dreams, considerable tossing and turning, and bouts of nausea. The morning was cold, an icy wind giving the nod to a coming storm. *I have no one to call on for help. How will I fight this off, keep the fiend from living in this house.* Getting the fires lit took her mind off the problem and she and Carrie actually had a good meal before leaving for the Thorndyke office.

"AH, MRS. CREIGHTON, EARLY AS USUAL," BEN Thorndyke said. "I have not made complete sense out of those ledger books you have put together, but I've most enjoyed what you call the bottom line." His smile radiated through the large outer office of the main building. "Before you start this morning, let's step out to my office for a little chat, eh?"

Irene Creighton shuddered just a bit at the words but gave an effort at a smile and followed the large gentleman out into the impending storm, across the open field, and into his office. She left Carrie with Gerald and Beverly. *Does he know about what Judge Petrini wants to do? Is he going to cancel out contract? Will it never end?*

"I've been in contact with Claude Atkins, the county attorney and Constable Tobias Kennedy concerning your son, Jeremy. I can't find the words to describe my feeling about what Judge Petrini wants to do. I've followed this situation closely because of my personal feelings about your late husband. Sit down, Mrs. Creighton, and relax. Regardless of the outcome, you will remain my company's keeper of the books."

"Oh, my God," Irene said, almost falling into the chair. The fireplace was burning hot and Ben threw another log in. "I'm more frightened, Mr. Thorndyke of what that monster might do if he is forced to live with us. Carrie has some terrible memories that must not be enlarged, sir. I can't let that boy back into our lives. I can't."

"I've helped write a letter that will be presented to the governor at some point in the next few days. Petrini, I'm afraid, is of the school that believes children cannot commit evil and doesn't see the horror of Jeremy's ways. The boy is made in the image of Ed Creighton and I'm afraid Creighton and Petrini were drinking friends. Petrini is in no position to even hear the complaint more or less pass judgement on it.

"He and Creighton were too close. According to Claude Atkins, Jeremy called the judge Uncle Tony during his questioning and after the first hearing. The governor will not enjoy hearing that."

"That's the first I've heard of it, too," Irene said. "Uncle Tony?" She was trying to remember if she had even heard her late husband mention anyone known as Anthony Petrini. "I've never heard Petrini's name mentioned. This is all new to me."

"Most of us in the business community knew Ed Creighton was a heavy drinker and played rather loosely with territorial laws. He and Petrini were rather close."

Ben Thorndyke sat back in his chair, a half-smile on his face. "Did you know the governor was one of my best salesman before he got into politics? Covered the Snake River Valley south of the Columbia. A good man."

She looked at him and wondered just where this conversation was going. *I'm lost, in a dream that has no ending, just one major problem after another. Creighton's treatment of me wasn't considered criminal but taking a bottle of rum was. Jeremy's attack on a little girl isn't considered a crime? And Mr. Thorndyke is a close friend of the governor.*

"What can I do?" Irene almost whispered.

"Hopefully we won't have to worry about an answer to that question," Ben said. "As far as you and Carrie? Just continue as you have been. You're a strong woman, Mrs. Creighton, and right now you have many friends willing to step in and fight for you."

It was hard for Irene to understand that she had any friends at all. After all, she thought, she was the woman who shot her husband. Having Ben Thorndyke as a client was one thing. Was this powerful Oregon businessman also a friend? Was Constable Kennedy to be considered a friend? And, she was certain she had never met County Attorney Atkins more or less the governor.

"Thank you, Mr. Thorndyke. I'll have these books all straightened out in the next day or two and we'll go over everything, line by line. I think you'll be pleased."

CHAPTER 13

"I've read all this, Mr. Atkins. What you have written and what Judge Petrini has written it seems are not about the same case. Have we two cases here? What you are discussing in your report is not the same as what Petrini has written. You're portraying what young Jeremy Creighton allegedly did was a heinous crime. The judge is discussing a childish prank."

"That is the problem, sir." Atkins took the cigar offered by Territorial Governor Henry Raymond, late of Rhode Island. Raymond was a salesman for a large manufacturer of commercial fishing equipment, such as cable, hawsers, metal pieces, and such who moved west because of the opportunities offered in Oregon Territory. After arriving he became a staunch supporter of the president who favored the man with this appointment.

Atkins and the governor were alone in the office for more than an hour before they emerged. "The strangest mishmash I've heard in a long time, Atkins. You tell Thorndyke for me to take that woman under his wing until I've had a chance to investigate this. A child sexually attacking another child is nothing but a childish prank?" He stood tall, shaking his head.

"That woman may have saved other children by her persuasive handling of a cast iron frying pan, Mr. Atkins. I'll put a stay on Petrini's order and you'll be hearing from my office in good time."

"Thank you, Mr. Governor." Atkins faced a long two-day journey back to Brookside. The man suffered from what was called consumption, his lungs constantly filled with liquid. He was in the timber business, spent most of his time outdoors in wet cold weather adding to his lung problems. It was his father who forced the younger Atkins to study law, but it was the timber business that paid for it.

Between a fierce winter storm, blown down trees, and rock slides, the trip turned into a four day adventure, leaving the man exhausted and sickly on his arrival. Rain and snow pelted the traveler day and night with no let-up. It was uphill for half the journey and downhill for the rest, but always in mud and slushy snow.

"I've been wet and cold for four days," he said to his wife as she helped him out of wet clothing. "My cough is much worse. Maybe you should fetch the doctor." Atkins was never a strong and healthy man, often down for days at a time during the wet, cold winter months. "I'm having a hard time breathing."

"I'll do that as soon as I get you in a warm bed." Syble Atkins was ten years Claude's junior, twice as strong, and always the optimist of the family. Atkins was unable to father any children, a frustration Syble had trouble with. She longed for the cacophony of a houseful and had, instead, a whimpering and sickly husband.

Despite his failure, she almost idolized the man, his knowledge, his humor, and the fact that he owned great tracts of heavily timbered land in Oregon Territory. "First, some hot beef broth, then I'll scamper for Doctor Winslow." She had two hot bricks wrapped in wool that she tucked under his blankets. "Hop in, Claude before they cool off."

While those in California grubbed about for flecks of gold, the astute in Oregon sought tall, straight timber. Great forests of fir, spruce, pine, and cedar stood as beacons of wealth, and Claude Atkins and his lovely bride would never go hungry a day because of his foresight in picking up several sections of timber land.

Doctor Winslow met Syble Atkins at the door and ushered her in. "You are slightly askew, Mrs. Atkins. What can I do for you?" The doctor always said what was on his mind regardless of how it might affect whoever was involved. Blunt and to the point. Sybil let the rude comment pass by with no retort.

"Mr. Atkins just arrived back from Oregon City and is in frightful condition,

Doctor. He's been in this storm for four days, is half frozen and coughing hard. I'm frightened, Doctor."

"He has bad lungs, Mrs. Atkins. I've mentioned it before, with consumption, the man shouldn't be living in this moist and cold climate," the doctor said. He was filling a small bag with medicines and said he would be along shortly, and to get back home, which Syble did.

What was he doing out in weather like this? In his condition? Some people simply won't take care of themselves. He needs to move south, way south, and get his lungs dried out. Consumption and living in Oregon. There was a distinct harrumph as the doctor left his office for the short walk to the Atkins' home.

Every street and pathway in Brookside became a quagmire every time it rained, and it was the rain that made the place a delight. Good ground with good water coupled with hard work made for successful farms, ranches, and backyard gardens. One still had to negotiate one's way through deep mud.

Rain mixed with ice sliced through the air, which was pushed along at near gale strength. The doctor knew snow would come a little later in the afternoon, when it cooled some. Syble let him in and showed him to the bedroom. A small Ben Franklyn fireplace had the room warmed and Atkins was sipping another cup of beef broth.

"Ah, the good Doctor," the county attorney said. "Afraid I've overdone it a bit this time."

"Yes, you have. What on earth would make you want to be out in this foul weather? Was it that important?"

"It's always important to get home, Doctor." He looked at Syble and smiled. "With such loving warmth waiting for me, I'd fight lions and tigers to get home."

Syble smiled and touched Atkins' cheek. Doctor Winslow said something very low as a mutter, which brought chuckles from Atkins. "Fill me with medicines, good Doctor. I'll need to be at my desk soon."

"I wish your desk was in west Texas instead of Oregon Territory," Winslow said. "You'd live longer."

"They don't grow trees in west Texas, Doctor," Atkins joked. "I'm a tree man. I'll always be a tree man."

"Were you in Oregon City because of the Creighton boy? Petrini is a fool. That boy should have been hung the second they found out what he did."

"We don't hang children, Doctor, but you're right about Petrini. And you're right about why I was in Oregon City. Had a long talk with the governor about the situation. That boy cannot be allowed to move back into society. He's a menace."

"What I've heard," Syble said, "is that he didn't even know what he was doing was wrong. That's a shame."

Doctor Winslow's face told a long story about his background, where women did not inject themselves in mens' conversations. He grumped and scowled at Sybil, as if saying, how dare you say anything while men are talking. Atkins's face however told the opposite story. "You're right," he said. The smile said he appreciated his wife's comments.

THE ORDER FROM THE GOVERNOR INFURIATED THE JUDGE but it also left him helpless. He was forced to put aside the case until further notice. The order also allowed Irene to live in a somewhat more peaceful situation. Life was flowing through calm waters even though everyone knew the rapids existed downstream.

She and Carrie arrived home one evening to find an envelope attached to her front door. "From the Hoagland's," she muttered, opening the missive. "My goodness." She and Carrie moved to the kitchen where she hurried to get the stove lit. It was another frightfully cold day and she swore she could see ice on the inside of the windows. It didn't take long for the room to warm up and Irene sat down to read the letter.

Carrie had moved to the living room to light the fireplace and Irene called for her to come back after it got lit. "We're going visiting on Sunday, Carrie. I don't think I've ever been to the Hoagland farm. They want us to come for Sunday supper. Won't that be nice?"

"Lucas told me it was big and muddy," Carrie said. "I like him, Mama even if he doesn't like your cookies. It's a big place, Lucas said, with lots of fruit trees and big fields of grass."

Irene's mind went back to her childhood days of neighbors being invited for supper, for having meals at other's places. Always gay and festive and so long ago. More than a lifetime ago, she thought, remembering it was proper to bring a gift when invited.

I've been out here on the frontier for so long I've forgotten what civilized life is like. In all this time the only visits I've made were with the Connor family. Ed Creighton had no friends and we never once visited anyone as a family. So sad. She couldn't get the ugly thought of how different this would be if she were forced to welcome Jeremy back to the family. *There would be no invitation from anyone.*

Sunday was just two days away, Carrie needed something crisp and pretty to wear, and she had no idea what she would wear. A girt? Oh, my. It would be furiously busy at the widow Creighton home for the next day or so.

CHAPTER 14

"I know I shouldn't worry over things I have no control over," Jacob Hoagland said, "but I do wish that spring would hurry itself along this year. One storm after another, heavy snow in the high country, and rivers and streams already over their banks. It's not right for a farmer to complain about too much water," he said. He chuckled to himself as he poured a cup of coffee. "Did Mrs. Creighton respond to your invitation?"

"Yes, for Sunday. She and Carrie will arrive about one and we'll have supper at three," Martha said. "I'll pull a corned brisket from the barrel and we have plenty of good winter squash left. Maybe a peach pie or apple pie after."

"Both," Lucas cried out. He had just come in and ran to the stove to warm up. "I love peach pie and apple pie. And peach cobbler, too."

"You like food, young man," Martha said, laughing and trying to tickle the boy. "My goodness, you've grown a foot this winter. It's all the time you spend with that mule and helping your father, I guess."

The boy was a good reader and Hoagland saw to it that he and Martha spent at least a couple of hours each day reading and doing numbers. Sometimes it was a fight but Lucas usually settled down and did his reading.

"What we need in Brookside is a school, Jacob. What would it take to organize a school? We always had schools back home." Martha was well read, had brought translated copies of Greek, Roman, French, and British classics when they made the long trek to Oregon Territory. She and Lucas read from them regularly. "How were the schools organized?"

"The villages were more compact where we grew up, Martha. There might be twenty or thirty families in this valley of ours but most of the farms and ranches are well out of the village proper. Something to think about, I suppose. We only went to school in the winter. There was too much work that needed to be done on the farm the rest of the year. It would be the same here. Lucas is getting a good education the way we're doing it."

"Yes, but what about the other children?" Martha asked.

"I suggest we don't try to answer that question."

Martha laughed and brought the coffee pot to the table. "The next time Commissioner Peabody rides through, ask him about creating a school in the county. I may bring the subject up at supper on Sunday," she mused. "I wonder where one looks to find a teacher?"

"Your mother is off and running, Lucas. I think it's time you and I found some late winter work out at the barn, eh?" He smiled at Martha as he got up. "You've got two days to work up your plot, my dear," he said, giving her a kiss on the forehead. "Our boy and I need to corral the waters of interior Oregon Territory."

"What does that mean, Papa?" Lucas asked. "Corral the waters."

"Mostly just a meaningless phrase, I'm afraid. See all that snow on those high peaks to our east?" He was pointing at majestic mountains not too far off. "That snow will start to melt soon and will rush to these lowlands. We need to control it to the extent that it waters what we want to grow, not washes out everything."

"Is that why we dig ditches?"

"Smart boy, Lucas." He took the next hour to explain how they have a series of impoundments that fill with runoff and are then drained over the summer in ditches to water the crops and fruit trees. "Trying to control mother nature is the hardest job any man has ever had. Sometimes we can, other times we can't."

"Like last year?" Lucas asked.

"I'm afraid so, Son, afraid so. This has been an exceptionally wet winter and we might be faced again with heavy flooding, but that work we did in the fall should protect us. Let's saddle up and take a ride around."

That got the boy excited, and it was a flurry of activity in the barn as Jacob saddled his horse and Lucas's new black mule. "Won't be long you'll be big enough to saddle Buddy by yourself, I think," Jacob said. He helped his son into the saddle and mounted his horse. The day was cold but without a wind it was a comfortable ride.

Jacob Hoagland watched his son ride the black mule he named Buddy and smiled. The boy was a good rider, sat with balance, no flailing arms, back straight, and attentive to his animal. "You and Buddy seem to be getting along well," he said.

"I love my Buddy," Luke said, quietly. "We want to go with you when you go hunting in the high mountains this year. I'm old enough now. I will need a good gun, though."

"Yes, you will," Jacob said. *Just a few short years from manhood. Last year he was a little boy. This year he's a big boy.* Jacob smiled, watched Lucas ride as if he'd had that mule for ten years or more. *I was his age when I got my first rifle and I can remember getting my first squirrel with it. And Martha's bringing us another little Hoagland, too. I'm blessed.*

There were three large impoundments that Jacob had dug to catch the spring thaw, and irrigation ditches spread out from them to the various fields. He used the existing terrain as much as possible and built simple earthen dams to hold the water back. He built gates that controlled the flow. These had to be manipulated by hand on a daily basis in the spring, summer, and fall. They were simple in design, but it took strength to work. Two stakes on each side of the flow were driven deep into the ground and twelve-inch planks laid up across the flow between the stakes.

The flow could be controlled by adding to or lifting out one or more of the planks. At the first impound Jacob was surprised to find it almost full. "This is how we corral the waters, Son," he said. They tied their animals to a tree and Jacob lifted one of the wooden gates from its rack in the dam, releasing a goodly flow into a ditch.

"A lot of this water will rejoin the creek below our house until we need to divert it for the fields in just a few weeks." Jacob used the same design as the dam for the diversions. "If you make this kind of work hard it will be hard and troubling, but if you make it more of a challenge, you and the water, who will win, it is enjoyable work."

"Seems pretty hard getting that plank out of there."

"Only for a few seconds," Jacob laughed. "What we need to think about, though, is when do we start flooding the field below us?"

"There isn't anything there," Lucas said. He had questions written all over his face. "Why put water on the land that doesn't have anything there?"

"Exactly," Jacob said. "So, we wait a few weeks until the weather becomes more spring like, and then we plant something so the water can make it grow."

Lucas stood quiet, watching the water flow out of the impoundment, looking down and across the broad meadows below, and smiled. "You're really smart, Papa."

"Farmers have been doing this for centuries, Son. Let's mount up and check the other ponds. It's a good day to be out like this. Nature can be a beast at times, and a sweet kitten at other times. It's knowing what to do at each of those times that determines if you'll succeed or not."

"Gotta be pretty smart to be a farmer," Lucas said, and Jacob just smiled, nudging his horse into a comfortable trot. "I sure do have a lot to learn."

Yes you do, Son. These next ten years are going to be the best in my life, I think. Jacob couldn't keep the smile off his face as they rode through the large and productive Hoagland family farm.

SUNDAY ARRIVED, FULL OF SUN AND LATE WINTER COLD, but no storm blowing snow and ice about. Irene Creighton finished Carrie's new frock the night before and had spent several days crocheting doilies for her gift to Martha. "I'm sure I don't have to remind you to remember your manners when we get to the Hoagland's," she said.

"No, Mama, I'll remember. I like Lucas. He's really strong, too. I like Gerald Thorndyke, too, but he isn't very strong. Not like Lucas."

Irene thought about that for a moment. "Gerald is probably even more strong than Lucas, honey, but in a different way. His strength comes from having to live with that bad leg of his. His strength comes from a strong will."

"I like both of them, but they are different from each other."

Yes, they are my sweet little girl. Another couple of years and you'll look on boys and men from different eyes. I just hope you have more sense than I when it comes to choosing a man. "Help me get the horse harnessed, Carrie, and we'll be off. *Why am I so nervous? My goodness, you'd think I'd never been invited to someone's home before.*

The thought caught her by surprise. It has been more than ten years since she had been a guest in someone's home. Almost from the time she met Ed Creighton. She never recognized how anti-social the man was until it was too late and then didn't do anything about it. "I have missed so much," she almost whispered.

One set of friends in the entire valley. Frank and Sabrina Connor. In all these years I have two friends. Jacob and Martha Hoagland are friendly acquaintances, not close as Frank and Sabrina. Maybe soon, though. Brookside is a thriving little frontier village filled with people. I've been here for years, and I know so few of them. There must be a village social life that because of Creighton we were not a part of.

The drive was only five miles but through some

lovely Oregon country and Irene let her mind rest, enjoying all that nature was showing her. First along the river, running high and fast from early run-off, and then into the rolling foothills of the high, rugged mountains.

"Look!" Carrie cried out as they emerged from a stand of trees. Up the hillside, less than fifty yards away, stood a magnificent elk. "Oh, Mama. He's so beautiful. What kind of deer is he?"

"He's not a deer, but an elk, honey. A big elk, too. Soon he'll regrow magnificent antlers and the girl elk will flock to his side." Irene had to laugh at her own comment. She didn't say, like girls always do. She had slowed the buggy down to a walk and the two watched the elk all the time the elk watched them.

"We need to do this more often, Mama. I've never seen anything so beautiful."

"You are right, honey. We really do need to get out and see the world. We've been cooped up like a couple of old biddy chickens. It'll be spring soon. Let's plan on going for little outings like this regularly." She couldn't help remembering how enjoyable the little adventure along the river on Christmas. "There is so much we've missed, little one."

They followed a fold in the countryside and the trail was along a tree lined stream toward the Hoagland farm. "Peaceful," Irene sighed, and Carrie found herself humming a little tune. An abrupt turn in the trail, around a great stand of fully mature fir trees, and there was the Hoagland farmhouse.

"That's not a very big house," Carrie said. "Our house is bigger than that." The trail took them across a bridge, through a small orchard of peach trees, and to the front of the house. Lucas bound out the door and down the steps to take the lead rope and attach it to the rack.

"Welcome," he called out. His smile was broad and open, and his eyes were shining. "May I escort you to our home? Mama taught me to say that."

"It's beautiful," Irene said. "Yes, fine sir, you may escort us to your home."

CHAPTER 15

"This is not within the governor's purview," Judge Anthony Petrini said. "Just who does this political sap think he is, telling me what to do. I'm the judge, not he." Petrini was stalking about in his cramped office behind the county courtroom on the second floor of the courthouse. The wooden complex was well built with split cedar and fir logs and solid fitted walls. Cold winds were kept out while hot summer air wasn't let in either.

Petrini was short, thin, balding, and shaking with anger. Growing up as always the smallest in any crowd, Petrini learned the art of negotiation at an early age and used this ability at every opportunity. It worked during the verbal and sometimes physical battles between the American Fur Company and Hudson Bay, and it's worked in his courtroom often. At the moment though, negotiation is the furthest thing from his mind.

"Mr. Olsen, you hustle downstairs and find the constable. I want him in this office within the next ten minutes. No excuses. Bring him to me." *Just who do these people think they're dealing with? The county constable, the county attorney, the capitalist humbugger, and the governor all conspiring to overpower the jurist? They'll rue the day.*

Sven Olsen, Petrini's clerk, hustled out of the office and down to the constable's office. "The judge is throwing a fit, Constable. Wants to see you right away."

"Must have gotten a letter from the governor, eh?" Olsen looked at him, wagged his head as if to ask, how would you know. "Has he thrown anything?"

"Well, uh, no, Constable, but he's used some fine language. What's this all about? I've seen him upset before, but this is close to rage."

"Good," Kennedy said. "Why don't you go on up and tell the old goat that I wasn't in my office, and no one knew where I might be, eh?"

"I can't lie to the judge," Olsen said.

Kennedy stepped out the door. "I'm not in my office," he said, and walked out of the building. "And nobody knows where I am," he chortled. *A spot of rum at Murphy's Tavern, some of Mrs. Murphy's fine lamb stew for lunch, and maybe a stroll along the river before I return.* He had his gnarled oak walking stick in hand, doffed his hat to a few of the town's ladies out for a stroll, and found Murphy's Tavern. The governor hadn't waited as long as Kennedy and the others expected before reaching his decision to put a stop to Petrini's court order.

Notes to Kennedy, Atkins, and Thorndyke had arrived that same day and Kennedy was expecting the call. *I wonder if that skinny little fool would turn Jeremy Creighton loose if he had attacked his daughter? His wife? His sister? Maybe I'll just ask him that question.* He greeted Murphy with a wide smile. "Good morning, Murphy. A fine winter's morning to you. Would you have a wee touch of rum for my cold bones?"

"I would, Tobias, yes I would. I might also have a barrel of whisky just arrived from an emerald isle we're familiar with."

"Then out with the rum, laddie buck, and in with the whisky. I was born somewhere between St. Louis and the Rocky Mountains, Murphy. Never seen the home country, only heard stories, but I can't imagine anyplace more greener than where we are."

"Oregon Territory is green, there's no doubt. As you, I've only heard stories. Speaking of stories, Mrs. Atkins stopped by for some stew for Claude. He's in a bad way, she said. Caught the grip coming home from Oregon City."

"Claude's been trying to die of bad lungs for a long time, Murphy. Hope he holds on long enough for us to finish our fight with Judge Petrini."

"Was what the Creighton boy did really that bad?"

"Aye, Murphy. If it had been your daughter, the boy would already be dead. That's how bad it was. Frank Connor has let it be known that if the boy is set free, he may not have another birthday. I've warned him about that kind of talk," Constable Kennedy said.

Glasses were filled a couple of times, great bowls of lamb stew were finished off in style, and the constable took a long walk back to his office. *Will it ever be spring again? I have had my fill of cold and mud.*

"Ah, Judge Petrini. What brings you down the long stairway to my humble office?"

"I'm going before the county commission tomorrow morning, Kennedy, and demand that you be removed from office. How dare you go to the governor and make complaint against me."

"Well, I'll tell you how I dare, sir. I dare because I'm a citizen of good character of the Territory of Oregon and the governor needed to hear what I had to say. Oh, and by the way, sir, I was elected County Constable not appointed. Surely, as a judge, you should know that."

He sat down at his cluttered desk and glared at the angry jurist. "Since you seem to believe in the letter of the law, what would your reaction have been if the Creighton boy had attacked your daughter?"

"I don't have a daughter, Constable."

"Hmmm. But you did have a wife. What if that boy had attempted something shameful with your wife?" Kennedy had no plans on letting up, would badger the little judge until the man relented. He got up to add wood to the stove.

"My Olga would have bashed the fool boy's head in, but all of that is conjecture, Constable. He was just a boy looking to discover the differences between boys and girls. All boys go through that stage."

"You and Creighton maybe, not I, nor any of my friends ever ripped clothing from little girls nor attempted to fulfill the act. No, judge, you're wrong and that boy needs to be away from polite society until he learns otherwise."

"I'll see to it that badge is taken from you, Kennedy." Petrini was red in the face, sweat ran off his bald head. "You, Thorndyke, and the governor will rue this day, Kennedy. Rue it, I say."

Kennedy chuckled and sat down behind his desk, opened the lower left-hand drawer and pulled a flask out. He reached behind him and took a tin cup from a hook and poured whisky in. "Did you have anything else on your mind? I plan to win my re-election in two years, Judge. The county commission can't do anything about that."

Petrini whirled about and slammed the door as he

left. Kennedy had to chuckle but also knew that this fight was a long way from being over. *I'd best make a social call on Claude Atkins and then drop in on Ben Thorndyke. Nasty times.*

"THAT WAS A WONDERFUL DAY, CARRIE, BUT THIS IS A NEW week and we've got to earn our daily bread. Hurry and get dressed."

"Boys get all the good stuff, don' they?"

"What's that about?" Irene asked.

"Lucas took me into the barn and showed me his mule. Mr. Hoagland gave him a mule for Christmas. I'll never get a mule, will I?"

Irene had to chuckle thinking about that. "Did you show Lucas your doll? I bet he'll never get one like yours?"

"Mama," Carrie said and then started laughing. "Maybe I should offer to trade him. I wouldn't want a smelly old mule, anyway. I love my doll."

They made the quick walk to the Thorndyke compound on a blustery Monday morning. "I've got two books that Gerald said he wanted to read and he's going to have one for me," Carrie said. "Did you know that Lucas is a good reader too? Will we visit them again?"

"I sure hope so," Irene said. They walked through the large Thorndyke farm and ranch supply store and to the offices in the back. "Good morning, Gerald. Is your father in yet?"

"He's at his office in the back. Said he wants to see you as soon as you got here."

"Thank you," Irene said. "Carrie, you and Gerald have a good day." She hustled out the back and across the broad field and smiled hearing the steam engine and massive hammers in the factory. *It certainly takes a lot of noise to make heavy machinery.*

"Ah, good morning, Mrs. Creighton, come in out of the cold." He helped her out of her heavy winter coat and got her settled in front of the fire. "More snow is on the way, I'm afraid. I've got good and not so good news this morning."

"About Jeremy? I've been terribly worried that they will force me to take him into our home. I can't do that."

"The governor, as I expected, set aside Judge Petrini's ruling on the matter. That's the good news, but I'm afraid that's not the end of the problem."

"Oh, it must be. It must," she said. "Why do you say it's not the end of the problem if the governor put an end to the ruling?"

"Petrini is asking the territory's high court to rule on the governor's decision. That will at least be months away so in the meantime Jeremy will remain at the boy's ranch. Petrini's an angry and mean man and will do what he can to get his way. This isn't over, I'm afraid."

He paced around the office, stared out the window, started to light a cigar and changed his mind, and finally sat down behind his desk. "I wonder if it might be time for me to have a little visit with the judge?" He was talking more to himself than to Irene. "Well, let's check out these ledgers you've created. Fascinating, and you've actually got me where I understand what some of it means." There was hearty laughter, and he slapped his desk top, too. "By Jove, Mrs. Creighton, I almost like bookkeeping now." The laughter was genuine, and Irene couldn't help herself, and joined in.

It was less than two hours later the two emerged

from the hide-away office and walked through the factory and around to the front of the store. "I take great pleasure walking through the factory," Thorndyke said. "To watch raw iron and steel, great stands of timber turned into machinery for farming, timbering, transportation, gives my heart a big charge."

"Isn't that Ike Connor at the forge? He's too young to be working like that."

"That boy is going to be the best blacksmith I've ever had working for me one day soon. He's a natural, and no, a boy needs to learn his craft when he's young. He's an apprentice, Mrs. Creighton. When he comes out of our program, he will be a full-fledged blacksmith and metalworker. He spends four hours a day learning his metal work, and then goes home. Did Creighton ever talk to you about Jeremy learning a trade?"

"Never," Irene said. She was watching Ike hammer some red-hot metal, slowly forming it into a spike. *Mr. Hoagland talked for some time about how Lucas was learning how to be a farmer and I'm watching Ike Connor learn how to be a metal worker, but Ed Creighton never once mentioned how Jeremy would fit in this world of ours.*

"Jeremy would be about the right age to learn a trade or craft," Ben Thorndyke said. Irene had a different thought than learning a trade or craft. Creighton was a criminal. Maybe that's what he was teaching his son.

"I'm going to see the judge and then make a trip to Oregon City. Spread some good Thorndyke business around the capitol city. We'll get together when I get back. I'm taking Gerald with me. Your books have already shown me where I'm overspending in a couple of places. Keep it up, Mrs. Creighton."

Irene picked up Carrie and they stopped at the

bakery for some sweets on the way home. "Have a good day?" She asked.

"I did, Mama. Gerald showed me some books he has on ships and boats. He really knows a lot about boats. He even made a model of a big three masted sailing ship, the kind that moves cargo and people from Boston to San Francisco."

"You're really excited about that, aren't you?" Irene was surprised at the girl's reaction.

"He wants to go to sea, Mama, but his mother doesn't want him to. He says his mother is afraid his bad foot would keep him from being able to."

"You two have some interesting conversations," she said. The snow started blowing about before they reached the front door. "Let's get those fires lit, young lady. It's going to be a cold night, I'm afraid."

It was a two block walk from the Thorndyke compound to the courthouse and Ben had to pass by Claude Atkins home on the way. He was about to pass by when Tobias Kennedy approached from the other direction. "Good day, Constable. Get that letter from Henry? He made the right decision."

"Yes, and I've already had my first confrontation with Petrini. On my way to check up on Claude. Those lungs of his will kill him soon, I'm afraid."

"I'm on my way to see the judge now. Tell Atkins to get well. We need him," Thorndyke said. The two men shook hands and went on their way. After just half a block Thorndyke decided he had nothing to say to the judge, would do better talking with the governor and others in Oregon City and turned for his home to pack.

Petrini was prowling around in his cramped office,

hands behind his back, head hanging down, giving long thought on how to deal with this set-back. *Henry Raymond has no business sticking his nose in my business. Just who does Ben Thorndyke think he is having the governor get involved in something that is purely the court's business? Claude Atkins needs to die and get it over with.*

The more he paced the angrier he became until he bumped his knee on the corner of his desk and had to sit down. The pain took away some of the anger, but not all. *It all started when that Creighton woman killed her husband and Kennedy didn't do anything about it. That was purely a crime of passion. She should have been hung.* He sat back thinking about that. Why wasn't she locked up? Hung? Who is behind this? The governor? Thorndyke? The constable?

This is all a conspiracy to make me look bad, to create a situation from which I could be set down from the bench. They are using that woman to eliminate me, but for what end?

Petrini let people believe that he was not a drinking man, didn't approve of it at all, and when the constable drank right in front of him, inside the courthouse itself, Petrini knew the man had to be relieved of his office. Now, it was becoming clear that it was those in favor of open alcohol laws who were behind the conspiracy. Ah, but which conspiracy?

That must be it. They have to get me out of office in order to make Oregon Territory an open territory for the free impor- tation and distilling of alcohol and they are using that poor, dear little boy as their primary tool. I'll stop them. They won't have their vile distilleries in this territory. Demon rum will not rule Oregon. The laughter would have seemed out of place to most who heard it.

A plan slowly formed that included the loss of posi- tion for Tobias Kennedy, loss of freedom, maybe even death for Irene Creighton, and the loss of business for Ben Thorndyke. *Thorndyke is looking to open distilleries here and in Oregon City, I know it, and Kennedy is helping him. All because that woman killed our good territorial land commissioner. And his son is paying the ultimate price. Not while I'm judge. I must eliminate those involved. Who first?*

CHAPTER 16

Irene was at the kitchen table surrounded by Thorndyke ledgers, bills of lading, charges, payments, and reams of paper. "This man is involved in more businesses than I've ever heard of," she murmured. "Every one of them is successful, which in itself is amazing." She was about to get herself another cup of coffee when there came a knock on the door.

She quickly put everything together and covered it. Someone's private business is just that. Private, she thought hurrying to the door. "My goodness. Sabrina, come in, come in. It's freezing out there. You must be frozen to the bone."

"Frank is picking up some equipment from Thorndyke's and I had him drop me off. I haven't seen you since Christmas, Irene. You look wonderful."

"I've been so busy with my new business. Let's sit by the fireplace. I'll bring coffee and some sweet rolls I picked up from the bakery. It's so good to see you. I saw Ike at Thorndyke's factory. He's an apprentice? Amazing."

The fireplace was hot, and Sabrina stood in front of it

for several minutes enjoying the warmth. "I've never seen him so happy," she said. "He has his own tools, has built a forge with his father's help, and is growing as strong as a mule. We got a note from Mr. Thorndyke that said when Ike finishes his apprenticeship, he will have a full-time position if he wants it. Amazing."

"He looked more like a man than a boy. How is Edith?" They were walking into the kitchen, all the time talking.

"I'm afraid she'll carry some dark thoughts and secrets for a long time, but she's doing better than I expected. Carrie?"

"Upstairs reading. She's doing well. It's been difficult for both of us. We visited with the Hoagland's last Sunday and she spends quite a bit of time with Gerald Thorndyke when I'm working at the compound. We're more social than I've been since arriving in Oregon years ago. I had no idea how Ed Creighton kept us locked up, so to speak." She brought the coffee pot to the table and poured for the two of them.

"It's what's happening with Jeremy that I'm most concerned about right now," she said. "Judge Petrini has ruled that Jeremy didn't commit any crimes, that what he did was just being a boy. Petrini wants to force me to take Jeremy back into our home," Irene almost broke down saying that, dabbed at her eyes but couldn't look Sabrina in the eye.

"That's horrible. What are you going to do?"

"Governor Raymond put a stop to the order, but Ben Thorndyke doesn't think it will last. That boy is not coming back to this house." She spat out the angry words. Anger replaced the sadness. "I'll not have him anywhere near Carrie."

Sabrina sat back, shocked at what she heard. "I'm sure

Frank doesn't know anything about this, or he would have said something." She was frightened at her next thought. *What will he do when he finds out?*

"All this in just the last week or two," Irene said. "Mr. Thorndyke is friends with the governor and he's on his way to Oregon City to try and get the governor to make the stay permanent. Judge Petrini is a mean old man who loves boys and hates women. Boys can do no wrong and the ills of the world can be traced to women, he says."

Frank Connor arrived shortly to pick up his wife and Irene stood at the doorway watching them leave for their farm. *That man won't like what she's about to tell him. What happened to their daughter was just a boy having some fun? Petrini might need an armed guard.*

THE JUDGE DID NOT COME INTO HIS OFFICES FOR TWO DAYS and Court Clerk Sven Olsen reported the matter to Constable Kennedy. "This is most unusual, Tobias. Most unusual. The judge never misses court, even when he's sick or has a cold, he shows up. I'm worried." Sven was a thin young man, intense at times, overbearing often. In the courthouse he was the voice of the judge. He told those few he called friends that his goal was to be a frontier lawyer and Petrini was helping him.

"I'll check on him, Sven. He's been under a strain with the governor putting a stay on his Jeremy Creighton order. I'll let you know what I find out." *Interesting. I wonder why Sven didn't check on the old man himself? Probably of afraid of him. The judges temper will lead to trouble someday.* Kennedy found it strange that Olsen waited two days to say something.

Olsen went back to the court offices and Kennedy grabbed his heavy bearskin coat for the short walk to

Petrini's home. *Coldest day of the year and I'm not heading to Murphy's for Irish whisky, I'm heading to see a grouchy old judge who is probably sick with the flu and now I'll be sick, too. Ah, well,* Kennedy chuckled, *it's our lot, isn't it? We decided to wear the badge, didn't we? And of course, we can stop at Murphy's on the way back, can't we?*

There was no answer after Kennedy pounded on the door several times. *The man doesn't drink is what Sven said, that's not the stories I've heard. Maybe he's not even home.* Kennedy tried the door and found it unlocked and stepped inside. "Cold," he muttered. There was no fire in the fireplace, the kitchen stove was cold to the touch. He called out a couple of times and got no answer, found the stairway and went up to the second floor. "It's Constable Kennedy comin' to see you," he cried out, and again got no answer.

There were two doorways on the left and one on the right along the hallway. The first door on the left opened to an empty room, and the second opened to a small office with a wall full of law books and a desk. When he opened the third door he shut it back immediately and reached for his handkerchief.

"My God," he murmured, stuffing the rag around his nose and mouth and stepped back into the cold room. Petrini's body, naked to the world, was sprawled across the bed. The back of his head was smashed by a four-pound metal worker's hammer, which was on the floor, propped against the bedstead. The heavy instrument covered in blood and bone.

"My, God," Kennedy said again. He took in the whole scene, took special note that Petrini was naked and there was no sign of a fight. "No bruises or cuts," he muttered. "Interesting that the body is cold and the blood congealed," he said and stepped back into the hallway, shutting the door. Downstairs he saw no signs of breaking in, all the windows were secure, the front and back doors were not locked but also not tampered with, and it didn't appear that anything had been searched. He closed the front door and hurried to Doctor's Winslow's house.

This certainly changes things for Mrs. Creighton. Many will make her a suspect since she killed old Ed Creighton with a cast iron frying pan. Whoever did this will be covered with blood but would have had lots of time to clean up. How many enemies did that angry old man make in the last several years.

The storm was raging, winds strong enough to blow a man off his feet, strong enough to fling loose material dangerously through the air, strong enough to topple fully grown trees, some of which were toppled.

"Doctor, I'm sorry to break in on you like this, but it is important. May I come in?"

"Yes, Tobias, of course, and close the door. Sounds like my house may take flight at any moment. You look terrible, Constable. What's the matter?"

"It's Petrini. He's been murdered, Doctor. I hate to ask this, but you must come with me to his home and verify the death and cause."

"Murdered? Are you sure?" Winslow pulled his heavy winter coat from a rack.

"There's no doubt in my mind, Doctor. His head has been bashed in by a heavy hammer and he's been dead for some time, I'm afraid."

Winslow wasn't a large man, and it was a struggle getting the few blocks to the judge's house. The wind threatened to send the good doctor down the street more than once and it was Kennedy's bulk that kept him upright. "Miserable weather," Winslow said several times.

102

"My God, yes, Constable, this is definitely a murder," he said. "Looks like he was hit from behind more than once. Whoever did this is large and was wearing gloves." Winslow continued his observations. "Look at the boot prints in the blood and how much damage that hammer did. Two distinct blows. The first one was all that was necessary, though."

"He's not been to the courthouse for two days, Doctor. Would that also be about when he was killed?"

"I'd say, since he has no clothes on, that he was killed three days ago, probably at bedtime. You'll be looking for a large person, but I can't speculate past that," Winslow said.

"Hmm," Kennedy said. "There are so many that he has treated roughly but this is so brutal, it must involve hatred not just anger. Those are vicious blows, Doctor. I need to gather some more physical evidence before I release the body. Can you make it back to your office?"

"I might need to stop off at Murphy's, Constable. I'll make it that far," he chuckled. "I'll notify Undertaker Salinski that you'll be calling on him."

"Thank you for everything, Doctor. I may have more questions and I would like your observations in writing, sir."

"They'll be on your desk shortly. My, God but this is brutal," he said as he slipped out the door.

KENNEDY HAD SEVERAL PAGES OF NOTES AND ROUGH sketches when he left Judge Petrini's for the undertaker's parlor. "Doc tell you I was coming?"

Shorty Salinski was thin, walked with a limp, and always appeared to be engrossed in something far, far away. "Yes, yes, Constable. What is this all about.

Winslow wouldn't say who or where. Not much I can do without that information, now is there?"

"There's been a murder, Shorty. That's why he didn't say anything. It's my duty, not his, to ask for your official work. I must ask that you not repeat what you'll see and hear. Judge Petrini has been killed. His body is on the second floor of his home. You'll need help retrieving it. Please don't discuss this with anyone until I finish my investigation."

"Don't know who did it, eh? Licentious old man has plenty of enemies."

"Licentious?" Kennedy asked, almost taken aback by the comment.

"Loves his little boys, I've heard," the undertaker said. "Well, best get on with it."

Tobias Kennedy made the short walk through driving snow to the courthouse. *I've got to let the commissioners know and Sven Olsen. Got to try to keep this as quiet as possible for as long as possible. We've not had a killing like this in many years. Not since the days of the fur company wars.* The thought caught him up short.

Petrini was involved in those disputes. No, too many years ago. Whatever brought this on, has to be relatively recent in nature. Everything leads back to the Creighton boy. He found County Commissioner Clyde Peabody and told him the bad news.

"The man has made some enemies over the years, Constable, but this is more than I might have expected. Any ideas of who might be involved? Probably not Mrs. Creighton, but she might have a reason."

"Aye, but she's not a suspect, Commissioner. No, I'm looking for a large person, probably a large man. He would have been bloody leaving the scene." Kennedy went up to the second floor of the courthouse to find

Sven Olsen and tell him the bad news. Olsen seemed to almost collapse, and Kennedy got one of the court people to help him into a chair.

"His is an appointed position," Olsen said. "The County Commission will have to appoint a new judge and that will take some time. We have cases scheduled. I've got a lot of work in front of me. He'll be missed, Constable, but not by all."

"Has he had recent threats, Sven? Anyone recently seriously upset with the man?"

"No physical threats that I know of. No secret little notes or anything. He's a strange man, Constable. Sees conspiracies where none exist, sees threats that don't exist. I haven't seen or heard any real threats."

I need to have a chat with myself over a glass of Irish and a bowl of stew. "Thank you, Sven. If you think of something, let me know." He fought his way back to Murphy's and a solid warm-me-up glass if Irish. "Loves his little boys?" he murmured a couple of times on the walk. *Where did Shorty get that idea? I haven't heard that. I wonder if this has anything to do with the Jeremy Creighton situation? The boy did call him Uncle Tony, after all.* He took a small table near the fireplace and sat down with his notes.

"I'll need a bottle and a bowl, Murphy. Stew goes in the bowl." He had a twinkle of the devil in his eyes, for sure. "This will be my office for the next few hours, I'm afraid."

"A terrible thing, Tobias. Murdering a judge? Terrible."

How the hell would he know that? Kennedy looked at the large Innkeeper, cocked his head, and almost whispered. "How would you know that?"

"Doc Winslow just left, Tobias. The whole village will know before supper."

"So much for a quiet investigation. He say anything else?" Kennedy's gnarled fists were locked tight, his brows knit, and his anger rising. *Told Shorty, didn't think I'd have to say anything to the doctor.*

"Said the scene was nasty. Think he used the word gruesome. Salinski been notified?"

Kennedy nodded wondering how long it would be before the real storm hit. "He's on the job, Murph." Kennedy poured a drink and took half of it without the usual banter. "I don't suppose a big person with bloody boots has been in recently?"

Murphy walked back to his bar with a gentle laugh. "At least not that I've seen, Toby."

Kennedy spent the next two hours going over his notes and sketches. *That type of hammer is used by those working with metal at forges, but is also used to drive spikes. Every farmer, rancher, and lumberman in the territory has at least one. Whoever did this is large and strong but there has to be a motive. What would drive someone to kill a judge? Money is often at the heart of these types of killings, but reputation is also a form of wealth. Has he held someone's reputation in the balance with a decision? Too many questions.*

His notes indicated that whoever it was, was probably well known by the judge. *He was naked, ready for bed. Was someone hiding in his bedroom waiting for him? Did the judge always leave his doors unlocked? Or was he naked waiting for someone?* Kennedy was good at reasoning, could see many questions that eventually would lead him to the killer, but not quite yet. *I need to know some of the more recent cases the judge has heard. The Jeremy Creighton case is one that would generate this level of anger, and even though we know that Irene Creighton is capable of murder, she didn't kill the judge. But was she involved? What other cases would generate this level of violence? I think Mr. Olsen and I need to have another long chat.* His notes, filled with questions that needed answers were in one pile, his notes on what he saw and found at the scene were in another, and the page he had marked, suspects, stood blindingly blank.

CHAPTER 17

F rank Connor and Sabrina were having coffee in their kitchen when Ike came in. "Have you heard the news?" He asked. He worked at the Thorndyke factory half a day and did his chores and studies the other half. "Judge Petrini was murdered. They found his body yesterday." He was almost shaking in his excitement.

"Calm down, boy." Frank Connor took a quick glance at his wife sitting across the table from him. Connor wanted to say something like, serves him right, but held his tongue. "Petrini? You're sure that's what you heard?" Ike nodded and wrapped his strong arms around his mother. "And you're sure the word murder was being used?"

"It was Constable Kennedy himself who came to the factory to tell us," The boy said.

Connor remembered his reaction when Sabrina told him what the judge had done, how he had cursed and said the man needed to die. He had lost his temper, said that if Jeremy Creighton was allowed to go free that the judge would pay a high price for his actions.

"You're in the middle of things in town, any talk about who might have done it?" Connor asked. *She's looking at me with a big question in her eyes. Does she really think I could kill a man?*

Sabrina watched Frank's reaction to what Ike was saying and wondered if he had anything to do with the murder. *Frank was so angry, spitting those terrible words out, but that was anger, not rage. He couldn't kill another man, could he?*

The Connor's daughter Edith came downstairs and climbed in Ike's lap for a welcome home hug. "No," Ike said. "Some people think it was Mrs. Creighton. That's crazy talk," the boy said. "I'm hungry."

Sabrina pulled a large piece of pork from a Dutch oven and sliced some for the boy. She heaped his plate with potatoes and covered it all with gravy. "Want some bread?" He nodded vigorously making her chuckle. "Silly question, eh?"

"You work awfully hard, Son. What else did you hear?" Connor asked.

"Constable Kennedy came to the factory looking at everyone's tools. Some say the judge was killed with a four-pound hammer, but it wasn't one from the factory. They were all accounted for."

"Don't most of the men mark their hammers? I know you've marked yours."

"Sure, but the constable counted all of them anyway," Ike said. "Can I have more, Mom?" His platter was empty.

"I think we need to raise more hogs, Frank," Sabrina laughed. "That boy eats at least one a week, all by himself."

"What did Irene Creighton tell you about Petrini's order?" Frank asked. "I can't imagine her being involved, but you can bet Kennedy does. And others in town."

"What she was most interested in was Ben Thorndyke going to Oregon City to talk with the governor. Governor Raymond put a stay on the judge's order. I doubt if he even knows about the murder, though."

"The stay would end that situation," Frank mused. Frank couldn't think of any other high-profile cases that might provoke a murder. There were always arguments over land and water, over roads and access, but these shouldn't create such anger or hatred that would lead to murder.

"Let's work on irrigation ditches this afternoon, Ike. Spring planting is just around the corner, boy."

"MORNING, SVEN, NEED TO TALK SOME," CONSTABLE Kennedy said, poking his head in the court clerk's office. "Any word from Oregon City on a replacement for Judge Petrini?"

"No. That has to come from the county commission, not the governor. Judge Adamson from south of here will handle things as a visiting judge. We're already way behind on hearings. Do you have anything new?"

"No, I don't. I found some recent writing by the judge while going through his desk, about a conspiracy of what he called, leading men, to build distilleries and distribute alcohol through the territory. Do you know anything about that?"

"Petrini was dead set against drinking, Constable," Olsen said. Kennedy looked at him with questions written all over his face. *How can he look me in the face and say something like that? Petrini drank like a fish as do most of his friends.*

Olsen continued, not paying any attention to Kennedy. "This conspiracy talk is new. There's more than one liquor distillery in the territory now. Beer, wine, liquor is made in many places. I'm afraid I don't understand. Did he include any names?"

"If he did, I wouldn't be telling you or anyone else." Kennedy frowned at the question and continued. "Other than the Creighton case, which I guess is moot now, what other big cases are pending?"

"The judge was furious at the interference by you, County Attorney Atkins, and Ben Thorndyke in the Creighton case. He was planning a trip to Oregon City to let the governor know he didn't appreciate his interference, either. Petrini has always had a soft spot for boys, and when those charges were made against a boy he considered his nephew, he was in a rage."

There we are again. A soft spot for boys, and Jeremy Creighton calling him uncle, Kennedy thought. "Why would Petrini have a soft spot for boys?"

"He said he was badly mistreated himself when he was a boy," Sven Olsen said. "He was a run-away at ten, is what we have been told, because of the mistreatment. Whippings, made to do without meals, verbally berated often. It came from his mother and an aunt, according to the stories he told."

"So, he takes care of boys? How?" Kennedy asked. *His mother and his aunt beat him? And now he transfers that hatred to all women? And likes boys? I don't like where my mind is going.* Kennedy was glaring at Sven Olsen.

"There are families in the valley that get food from time to time, he helps with clothing, and is involved in holiday parties for boys. The man had a great dislike for women in general, and in particular those women who appear to be strong willed."

Kennedy was writing all this down as fast as he could and looked up from his desk to see a frown on Olsen's face. "What is it, Sven?"

"He wrote a petition to the governor and planned to give it to him personally. As you know, County Attorney Atkins, at your suggestion, refused to charge Mrs. Creighton with any crime in the death of Ed Creighton. The judge vehemently argued that the woman should be hanged."

"That's why the man should never have been appointed judge in the first place. Too opinionated to be a fair judge of people. Without a court hearing? He was going to petition the governor to do what?" Kennedy could almost see the scene in the Creighton kitchen the night the vicious old man was killed.

"To order the woman arrested, tried, and hanged. We tried to talk to him. Governor's can't do what he wanted, but he was determined. He and Creighton were close friends, you know."

"I've heard," Kennedy said. "You said Petrini didn't drink."

"That's right. Hated those that did. Wanted to have Murphy closed up because so many drank so much in his place."

"On the other hand, Sven," Kennedy said. He had an ugly frown spread across his face, "I've been told that Petrini and Creighton were drinking friends. That they were known to get together with a few other men at a hunting lodge and have roaring parties when they were supposed to be hunting meat for their families. That the Creighton boy, Jeremy, was often along."

Olsen sat back in his chair near the pot-belly stove with a surprised look on his face. "I don't think you've heard right, Constable." Kennedy looked at the man closely and wondered if he had been lied to, and if so, on which end of the question.

Creighton's son said Petrini and his father were drinking friends. Thorndyke mentioned the two men being drunk often. Olsen is holding the judge up as hating drinking, drinkers, and even the sellers of liquor. Are there two people here? One judge the drunk, the other judge the teetotaler?

"Sven, this is important. Are you sure about what you're saying about Judge Petrini and liquor?"

"Constable, Judge Petrini has even written about the evils of demon rum. The *Brookside Sentinel and News* has carried his commentary on liquor often. Surely you've seen those."

"I haven't," Kennedy said and thought to himself that he would certainly check that out. "All right, Sven. That's enough for now. You'd better get back to your work. I'm sure I'll have more for us to talk about soon. Thank you."

Kennedy sat back, holding his notes. "Leading townspeople, a boy who calls the judge uncle, say that Petrini is a heavy drinker and the judge's own court clerk says the man detests liquor and even writes commentaries against drinking in the local newspaper." His muttering continued and slowly just morphed into thoughts.

The man's an enigma. Was he killed for his like or his dislike of liquor? Was he killed because he took advantage of little boys? Was he killed because of some court case that someone disliked? Or is there something I haven't heard about yet? I need some straight talk with Murphy and his friend from the old country. Kennedy was chuckling as he slipped into his heavy winter coat.

CHAPTER 18

"A messenger just brought this from Brookside, Governor," an aide said, handing Henry Raymond an envelope. It was addressed to the governor and marked important. "Shall I wait?"

"Yes," Raymond said. He read the missive quickly, frowned, and jotted a note. "Take this to Ben Thorndyke at the Oregon City Hotel. Ask him to come to my office. He'll understand." Henry Raymond paced around the office, contemplating what the message might portend. There was always the question of British and Russian intervention in Oregon Territory. Again, this could simply mean the judge angered someone.

Communication between towns and villages on the frontier was slow and often unpredictable. From Brookside to Oregon City meant crossing a high pass and a single rider could make the run in three days if the weather was decent and the Indians were behaving themselves.

The aide left and the governor sat back in his large leather chair, lit a cigar, and gazed out the second floor window. "Is all of this connected?" He muttered and let his mind wander. *Petrini murdered? Thorndyke here about the Creighton boy? To have my stay made permanent? A boy committing adult crimes and his father killed by his mother? That little village of Brookside is interesting enough to warrant a governor's visit.* He had to chuckle thinking about it. Henry Raymond had been a first line salesman for Thorndyke before being appointed territorial governor. He knew well the village and many of the people and wondered just what was going on down in that lush little valley.

He could see the rolling foothills beginning almost at the banks of the river, lush and productive. Fields of corn, wheat, and grasses, great orchards of fruit, and the livestock. *Why, my goodness, there were great pastures filled with cattle, sheep, and fine horses. I've told more than one friend that valley is a paradise,* the governor thought.

Raymond remembered that it was the county attorney, the village constable, and a leading businessman who came to him about the Creighton boy. Now he finds out the judge in the case has been murdered. *There may just be more to this than meets the eye. Petrini was involved in the ruckus between the fur companies, but was never among the rowdies, the troublemakers. His line of troublemaking involved learning about his enemies secrets and playing on them. Has he delved too deeply into someone's secrets?*

"Ah, well," the governor said, an almost satisfied smile on his face, "those in Brookside will soon have their answers."

Ben Thorndyke read the note from Raymond and grimaced. "I hope this isn't connected to Mrs. Creighton," he murmured. He retrieved his coat and hat from a rack. "Tell the governor I'm on my way." Thorndyke was a big man and he struggled to get into his greatcoat, found a walking stick, and strode down from his second story hotel room.

His mind was filled with a thousand questions as he made his way to the Oregon Territory capitol. Kennedy was on the job in Brookside, as was Atkins, so from a law standpoint most of the questions would be answered. *I'll get what I can from Henry and leave out for home right away. At least the storms have let up some.*

"This is most unusual, Ben," the governor said. "Have threats been made? Is the Creighton boy's family involved?"

"Most unusual indeed, Governor. I'm afraid I know as much as you do. I've not heard of any threats other than griping from people losing a case and Mrs. Creighton is the only family the boy has. I'm sure she's not involved. I'll leave first thing in the morning," Thorndyke said. He was trying to put it all together and wasn't getting anywhere.

"Petrini was a strange man, Governor. He was a heavy drinker who wrote blistering articles about the evils of demon rum. He claimed that he never married, hated women and girls, but always had time for boys and their fathers. There are some that say he was married, once, and that the woman disappeared."

"He was appointed by a previous governor, Ben, so I don't know much about him. With the new law, it's up to the counties to name their judges. I received a demand last week from Judge Petrini that I see him on a visit he had planned. He did not ask for an appointment, he demanded one."

"That would be his way," Thorndyke chuckled. "Since the judge is dead, will you make permanent your stay on his order to drop charges in the Jeremy Creighton case?"

"It's in the works, Ben. I read what Constable

Kennedy wrote, what County Attorney Atkins wrote, and the interviews with Frank Connor and Irene Creighton. That boy committed heinous crimes. He needs to be in prison." He caught himself and continued, "but not before a fair trial. Will that farm for criminal boys hold him? He sounds like a hard case."

"That's the irony or problem in this situation, Governor. He doesn't think like a hard case, like a criminal. His father taught him everything he is accused of doing and doesn't understand that what he did was wrong. The boy was taught criminal activity thinking that was the proper thing for a man to do. The father was the criminal."

"And the mother took care of that problem, eh?" Governor Raymond said. "Quite a family."

"Mrs. Creighton was as much in the dark as her son. Had no idea what was going on between the father and son. Only knew she was on the wrong end of brutality coming from her husband. She's now my company's bookkeeper and raising her daughter."

Governor Raymond shook his head and reached out for Thorndyke's hand. "Have a safe trip, Ben. Help find the murderer if you can and keep me apprised along the way."

"Thank you, Henry, I will. If you and the president get in a twit, your job will always be available." Warm laughter ushered Thorndyke out of the office.

TOBIAS KENNEDY WAS SITTING AT A TABLE NEAR THE kitchen at Murphy's Inn and Tavern, a bottle of Ireland's finest on one side and a deep bowl of lamb stew on the other. Directly in front of the constable was a pile of paper filled with notes and sketches.

"Just look at this mess, Murph. Somewhere in all this

is a killer's name, address, and next of kin." Murphy wagged his head, harrumphed some, and went back to his bar. "Ah, well, I'd best get on with it. Oh, and my manners. Say hello and praise the lamb stew when you see the Missus."

"Mrs. O'Reilly will be pleased to hear that," Murphy said. "You've a mess to go through."

The hammer used by the killer had no personal markings on it which would have solved part of the crime. Kennedy was aware that those who used this kind of hammer professionally put some kind of mark on the steel so all would know the owner. Not being marked might mean it was a farm or ranch tool Or, might mean it was company owned, not the user's personal tool.

"No," Kennedy muttered. "The company would have their mark on it, too." Taking each piece of evidence and using it to eliminate possible suspects would take a lot of time, considerable whisky, and great volumes of stew. "Because of a lack of a mark I think I can eliminate blacksmiths and their helpers and those working at Thorndyke's factories. Maybe. Need to go a different direction."

Kennedy looked around, realizing he was actually talking right out, not muttering, and scowled at the thought. "Boots." He said. The bloody footprints in the judge's bedroom were large and it appeared made by hob-nailed boots. "Maybe a woodsman? Or someone wanting me to think that?" He poured another bit of whisky in his glass and stared at his notes.

He sat still for a minute trying to picture the scene in the bedroom. The naked judge, his head bashed in, sprawled across the bed. A bloody four-pound hammer propped up and leaning against the bed. And bloody boot prints near the bed.

"That's it," he said, loud enough to catch Murphy's attention at the bar. "The bloody prints don't go nowhere. The killer took his boots off to leave. Did he throw them away? What else might be discarded? Got to get back and go over that property on the outside. Oh, Toby Kennedy you just aren't as smart as you should be, sometimes, laddie." He chuckled at his comments.

Kennedy downed the whisky, took a couple more large spoons full of stew, and struggled into his great coat. "Be back in a while, Murph," he said hurrying out the door. It was a quick two block walk. "At least no wind, snow, or ice to worry about. Oh, I hope my luck holds."

CHAPTER 19

C laude Atkins was sitting up in bed enjoying another cup of Sybil's beef broth. "I can feel spring, Sybil, you're nursing me back to health, and I'll be out in the trees again soon."

"I received a note from Ben Thorndyke this morning, Claude. He wants to know if you're well enough for a short visit. He just got back from Oregon City."

"Oh, yes. Yes indeed. Maybe you could get a message to Tobias Kennedy, too. I'll dress and be ready for them. I've been away from my duties far too long." Atkins owned large tracts of timber country but was elected Brookside County Attorney. He studied law because of his timber business and when he passed the bar, he was talked into serving the county. He told anyone who would listen he would prefer being out in the woods to being stuck in an office.

His coughing was not better nor was it worse than when he first went down. "I've been tied to this bed for two weeks, Sybil. That's long enough."

She nodded, thinking maybe two weeks this time but how many times has it been? She wasn't ready to be a widow, wasn't fully ready to be a full-time nurse either. "Have you ever given serious thought to selling your properties here and moving to a drier climate? I love Oregon, but if it meant getting you well, I'd certainly agree to our moving." Young, very attractive, Sybil has grown to love this sickly but very rich man. In the beginning, her attraction was probably more the security of the marriage, but over time it is now a real marriage.

"My father was a fir tree, Sybil, and my mother the rich earth of the forest floor. No, I'm a child of the timber." They were both laughing when someone pounded on the front door. Sybil hurried across the house to find Tobias Kennedy.

"Constable. We were just talking about you. Come in, please."

"I hope Claude is feeling better. That pass is hard enough to navigate without having to fight off Mother Nature, too." She helped him off with his great coat and ushered him into Claude's sick room. "There you are, sloughing off your duties, I see."

"Toby, come in, sit. Maybe a cup of coffee?"

"If it has a nip of rum, maybe so," Kennedy said, giving Sybil a big smile. "Thought I'd take a couple of your precious minutes to go over the Petrini case. Feel up to it."

"Yes, yes I do. Have you learned something?

"I don't think I have," Kennedy said. "It's perplexing and that's why I'm here. Sometimes when two people are working on a question an answer might be seen by one of them before the other. We have three big questions that must be answered before we can name the killer. Why was Petrini killed? Who owned or used the hammer? And whose boots were they that I recovered?"

Claude Atkins lay back on his pillows and stared at

the ceiling, coughing gently. "An answer to any of these questions could solve this little problem, I think. It is the 'why' part that intrigues me the most. Petrini was not a likable man, especially when he was drinking. And those little fables he had published in the paper were rot-gut at best. Pretending he didn't have a taste for John T. Barley Corn. Humbug. A dedicated drunkard was our fair judge."

Kennedy had to chuckle remembering how court clerk Olsen was positive that the judge never touched a drop. "Apparently Petrini and Ed Creighton were drinking friends. I've heard that from several. And the Creighton boy called the judge 'uncle'. What do you know about Petrini having young boys as friends?"

"Only if their fathers were drinkers, Toby. He considered it a pathway to manhood for the boys to be involved in some of the little outdoor adventures, such as sitting around a campfire drinking whiskey and telling ribald stories about bad women."

"How is it you know something about this?" Kennedy thought he was well attuned to the village's activities, but these revelations were all new to him. "I just heard about some of this in the last few days."

"Petrini had a great dislike for women, even girls, and felt it was his duty to see to it that all boys knew just how terrible women were. Most of the men in his little clique felt the same way, led by Ed Creighton. I've always found it interesting that it took Irene Creighton as many years as it did to finally end her life of terror." Atkins took a shallow breath, coughed and tried to continue.

"Petrini's younger life, from what I've heard was ugly. He was orphaned, left to relatives who didn't much want him, beaten regularly, and put out at first opportunity. I've heard more than one variation on this subject as well," the county attorney said. "Some say his mother beat him while others are sure he was an orphan. I think some of the stories were made up by Petrini himself."

Kennedy took the offered cup of coffee with a delightful aroma of good rum and sat back in his chair. "Everyone I've talked with has said the same things you're saying, Claude." Kennedy took a sip and smiled. "And yet I've not known a thing about most of it. I'm not a very good constable, I'm afraid. How could all this come to pass without me knowing?"

"If you weren't a fine constable, Toby, you wouldn't be sitting with me discussing this case," Claude Atkins said. "You said boots and hammer along with why. Let's get back to that. Why was Petrini killed? He had no liking for women so it wouldn't be a jealous husband or friend. Was it a case of he liked men?"

Sybil took in a quick breath. "Claude."

"Sorry, sweet lady but it does happen," Kennedy said. "But not in this case. I don't think Petrini liked anyone and few liked him." He didn't say anything but there was that terrible question of the boys that clouded his mind. Did he dare even bring up his thoughts on the matter?

"The men liked his liquor, Sybil." Atkins said. Toby gave him a quick look.

"No, Claude, I meant exactly what I said. There are men who like men, and these gatherings we've been discussing, well, it is possible."

Atkins took a quick look at his wife, nodded as if in agreement. "I have a file you need to see." He turned to his wife still standing in shock about what she heard. "Would you get a bundle of papers marked Imports from my desk?"

Sybil brought a large bundle to Atkins. "I've been on this trail for more than a year. Shipments of fine Virginia rum have been arriving at our ports and are being distributed before taxes are being paid. I'm afraid our recently departed jurist may be involved, may even be the owner of the operation." He handed a set of papers to Kennedy. "Page through these."

"I've just discovered that Ed Creighton was taking bribes of Virginia rum in his dealings as Territorial Land Commissioner and I recognize the label here." He pointed at a rendering of a label. "Was there more to their relationship than just drinking and hating women? How would this relate to his death, though? More questions, Claude."

"Take this file and spend some time on it, Toby. There are a lot of names. I'm afraid the questions on the boots and hammer will have to wait. I'm awfully tired."

"Oh, Claude, I'm sorry. I've just kept pushing, haven't I? Get your rest." He gathered up the voluminous file. "I'll see myself out, Mrs. Atkins. Thank you." Sybil was already at Atkins' side.

Back at the office Kennedy opened the file and started going through the many pages taking notes along the way, in particular, he noted names of men and boys. Some of the men involved with the judge had also recently became land owners in the valley, authorized by Ed Creighton.

"It's a long throw from bribing a land commissioner to killing a sitting judge," Kennedy murmured, closing the file. "Tomorrow is soon enough to hack my way through this. I need a chat with Ben Thorndyke." During the short, but middy walk to the Thorndyke compound he tried to understand how any of the questions could even be related. *Boots, hammers, illicit liquor, and a murdered judge. There's a big key in there somewhere and I have to find that key soon. If whatever it might be led to one murder, will another take place?*

"HELLO, BEN. HOW WAS YOUR TRIP TO OREGON CITY?" Kennedy had been to Thorndyke's little private log-cabin office many times and enjoyed it every time. *If I should find the pot of gold as Ben has, I'll have a nook like this to hide in, shy myself from the world.* He sat down in front of the fire and warmed his hands. "Spring can't be too far off, can it?"

"I've put my order in," Ben laughed. "It was a good trip but completely useless. Because of the murder I didn't really have to be there. Henry Raymond had everything under control. Anything new on Petrini's death?"

Kennedy spent a long time outlining everything he knew and looked at Ben Thorndyke with his unanswered questions. "There is one or more in this valley with all the answers. What is it that connects all of this that we know about Anthony Petrini to a murderer?"

"I think I would start by pursuing those questions that Atkins has opened about untaxed liquor, Tobias. Money, Constable. It always has some bearing on criminal activity. I've heard you say that more than once." He sat back in a heavy and well-built leather arm chair, lit a cigar, and took a long sip of whisky. "Some money is used for the benefit of society, Toby, while other money shanks that same society."

"I have a short list of names, Ben, that I would like you to go over. They are known drinking friends of Creighton and Petrini. They also appear to be involved in the untaxed liquor distribution scheme." He retrieved and unfolded a sheet of paper and handed it to

Thorndyke. "I recognize some of these names, but others are unknown. I don't even know if they live in the valley."

Thorndyke took the sheet and scanned it. "Hmm. Yes, I think I know most of these names. May I keep this and write out what I know about these people? I'll bring it to you first thing in the morning."

"I'll look for it, Ben, and have the coffee boiling when you get there," Kennedy said. It was a short walk to his home and he was in a better mood because of his visit with Thorndyke. "Maybe I'm finally getting somewhere." He was still half a block from his home when he saw a man running from his porch to a carriage. The man jumped on board and another man whipped the single horse into a hard gallop away.

Kennedy ran the half block to his house in time to put out a small fire that had been started at his front door. He stomped the fire out, scattered the kindling and smelled the distinct odor of whale oil, often used in lamps. *Well, now, I've stirred someone's nest, eh?* It was getting dark but Kennedy walked off the porch and got down on his knees to look at the prints of the man who ran away.

Hobnail boots. I've got to measure this print against the one I have. Later, as he cooked his supper, he realized he recognized the carriage into which the man jumped. *I've seen it more than once, but where? Whose carriage was that? Two men want me burned out, eh? I wonder if their names are on that list?*

CHAPTER 20

Ben Thorndyke sat back in his comfortable chair and looked again at the list of names Kennedy left with him. Just five in all, Ben was acquainted with four of the people. *Who is this fifth yahoo?* The first four names included two known drunks and wife beaters. *I'm sure Kennedy will put the fear of God in them, but I wouldn't count on either having the spine to kill a man.*

It was the fifth name that had Thorndyke's mind working. *Theodore Upton. I simply cannot place that name and I'm sure if he lived in our valley, I'd know him. Is he the brains behind the liquor imports?* Thorndyke let his mind play with that for a spell. It would be a motive for murder if Upton wasn't fair with the distribution of money.

In the often cold and wet climate of Oregon Territory, rum was often the choice to warm one's blood, and Virginia rum was always the first choice. For the more affluent, brandy would warm their blood. Supply of the fine rum was never equal to demand and a barrel of untaxed Virginia rum brought in a lot of gold. *Enough gold to kill a man?* Thorndyke knew the answer was a solid yes.

He wondered, then, who was cheating whom? Was Upton cheating and Petrini found out and challenged him and got his brains beat out? Or was it the other way around, Petrini cheating the others and someone was named executioner? *Our constable has his work cut out, I think.*

First thing the next morning Thorndyke walked among the men in the factory casually asking about a man named Theodore Upton. He got blank stares until he stopped to chat with Greg Farnsworth working some hardwood on his lathe. "Upton? Ne'er-do-well, Mr. Thorndyke. If you're plannin' on hiring the blotter, you'd do better to find a piece of scum in Portland."

"Tell me about this Upton, Mr. Farnsworth. I've never met the man."

"He works as a sawyer for one of the lumber mills. Heavy man with a foul mouth and always has a bottle nearby. Sotted most of the time, Mr. Thorndyke. Missing a finger on his left hand, and most of his teeth as well," Farnsworth laughed. "He's a loser, sir." Farnsworth stopped suddenly, as if in thought. "He's not allowed in any of the valley's bawdy houses. He's known as one who takes his problems out on women. Runs with a fellow named Slack Jaw something. Can't remember the name."

"Would it be Compton?"

"That's it, yes. Slack Jaw Compton. He was run out of Washington. Brits say he was an arsonist and killer. Has been around here for less than a year, I think. He and Upton have caused some trouble with the timber cutters."

"Thank you, Mr. Farnsworth. I appreciate your information. I won't be hiring either man," he chuckled, whacking Farnsworth on the shoulder. "Never fear, they aren't the sort I want around here."

Ben Thorndyke had a smile on his face when he walked into Tobias Kennedy's office an hour later. "Might have some information for you, Constable, if that coffee pot's hot."

"Hot and full, Ben. I could use some good information."

"A couple of those names you gave me have turned out not to be the type to start or operate a liquor scam of the type you outlined. Scum of the earth I'm afraid. This Upton fellow is large, mean, and ignorant and his running mate, Slack Jaw Compton is about equal. I don't see them running the operation, but that type of fellow is certainly capable of nipping the profits. According to one of my men, this Compton fellow is a known arsonist as well."

"Or killing the judge?" Kennedy asked. "Curious that, with the exception of Judge Petrini there aren't any others of, say, a higher intellect?"

"I'm guessing here, Constable, but I would say there either was or is someone we don't know about." Thorndyke took the offered coffee and sat down near the pot-belly stove. "It's a case of there was someone else, someone who actually ran this fraud, and somehow wasn't there any longer, it is possible these two ruffians might try a takeover?"

"Starting with eliminating the judge." Kennedy paced around the small office. "That's an interesting theory, Ben. Interesting. Who would have the intelligence to put together such an operation? Someone familiar with government operations, someone capable of bringing in important people, someone with connections."

"That's a fine description," Ben Thorndyke said. "I'd like to meet this man," he chuckled.

"I think you might already know him. I'm thinking Anthony Petrini had a partner and used men like Upton and Compton to do the heavy work. I'd put money on Ed Creighton being that partner."

Thorndyke stood straight up, almost spilling his coffee, and stared at Kennedy. "You've got it, Toby, yes."

"As close as the two men were, as both were heavy drinkers, and both knew the ins and outs of government, slipping barrels of rum in without paying duty and taxes wouldn't be difficult. When Irene Creighton killed old Ed, it stopped or slowed the operation and those two slum dogs decided to take over," Kennedy said.

Kennedy didn't say anything about the attempted arson at his home the night before, but it did fit into the picture he was drawing. "Of the two, Ben, which do you figure to be the one to make the decisions? Upton or Compton?"

"What if there's a third we don't know about who wanted a part of this lucrative liquor operation? What if those scoundrels were simply hired assassins? We're talking a lot of money, Kennedy. Somewhere in this valley there is a barn or large building where barrels of rum are brought, transferred into jugs or small kegs, and distributed through the territory. Every pub, saloon, and outlet has the product, Toby." Thorndyke's mind was on distribution, it was his business, and he could see the profits that would flow in.

"We've expanded this investigation considerably since you arrived, Ben," Kennedy chuckled. "Hiring someone to kill a judge might not be that difficult, I'll agree to that. Someone would have to know about the liquor scheme in order to want to be a part of it. Maybe not able to financially be among those who started the scheme, the fraud, but wanting to be a part of it."

"I think you're going in the right direction," Toby," Ben said.

"And when Ed Creighton was killed, this person saw his opportunity, hired the two thugs, and now holds the keys to the scheme," Kennedy said. He poured coffee for the two of them and laughed right out. "Well, we've solved this mystery, eh? Except for a very important part. We don't know who this great thinker might be."

"That's your end of the deal, Toby. I've got to get to work. Keep me informed, please." Ben Thorndyke walked to his factory, trying to put together what the two had discussed. *Someone walking among us has hired killers to assassinate a judge and take over a fraudulent distribution system. Who would be capable of that?* Ben of course wouldn't have been aware that those same thoughts reverberated in Kennedy's mind.

CHAPTER 21

"Papa," Lucas Hoagland cried out. He was riding Buddy, the black Christmas mule at a goodly clip into the farmyard. "Papa, where are you?"

"Easy there, Lucas," Jacob yelled coming out of the barn. He grabbed up the mule's headstall and got the animal calmed down as Lucas jumped off. "There are men in our old apple orchard, Papa. Two men and they yelled at me. One had a big knife."

"All right, boy, calm down and let's have it, nice and slow." He walked the mule into the barn and tucked it into a stall. "Sit, Lucas and take it slow, boy."

They sat on some stacked fence logs across from each other. "We were riding through the old orchard and I saw some smoke and wanted to make sure it wasn't something to worry about. Like you've always told me. Fire can do a lot of damage, so I rode toward it and found two men with a tent and campfire."

"Did you ride into their camp?"

"No, but they saw me and one started yelling bad things at me. I was scared, Papa. He was shaking his fist and started running toward me. The other man had a big knife and started running, too. I kicked Buddy hard and we raced back home. They shouldn't be there, should they?"

"No, they shouldn't, Lucas. Did you notice anything else?"

"They had a small carriage and a horse. There was a deer hanging from one of the old apple trees. That's our orchard, isn't it?"

"Yes, it is, Son. Let's you and me take a little ride into town and have a talk with the constable. I want you to tell him everything you saw." Jacob saddled his horse, got Lucas back in the saddle and the two rode out of the barn.

Martha was on the back porch as they rode up. "Stay in the house with the doors locked until we get back, Martha. Don't open the door to anyone," Jacob said, and he and Lucas rode off for the village, just five miles away. "You did right in coming straight to me, Luke. There have been more of these drifters coming through on their way to California. I think a lot of them are criminals, too."

The five-mile ride was quick and they walked into the constable's office. "Hello, Mr. Hoagland, Lucas. What brings you to town on this cold morning?"

They shook themselves out of their heavy coats and warmed their hands at the stove. "Might have a couple of drifters camping on my place, Constable. Lucas accidentally rode up on their camp and they threatened him with a knife. Thought it best if you handled the situation."

"Appreciate that, Hoagland. Always best if you don't take things into your own hands. Tell me about these two, Lucas. You rode right up on them? That could get dangerous fast, son."

"They were in our orchard and I saw smoke. I wasn't right in their camp. One man was really big and had a knife. The other said he was going to cut my heart out and eat it."

"Anything else?" Kennedy asked. *Sounds like they just wanted to chase the boy off.* He didn't chuckle at Lucas's comment. A young boy's imagination? Or somebody not wanting company?

"They had a tent and a carriage. It was a one-horse carriage and their horse was almost as black as my mule."

Kennedy sat a little straighter at those comments and looked the boy up and down. "The smaller of the two men, what did he look like?" Kennedy was afraid the boy would describe one of the men that Ben Thorndyke talked about just an hour before.

"He was tall and thin, had a long beard and his hair was tied back with a rag. He was really dirty and talked funny."

"Funny? How funny?"

"Like he couldn't pronounce his words right. His mouth was twisted when he yelled at me. He wore heavy boots. Both men did."

"I think I might know who you met up with, Master Lucas and I'm glad the two of you came to me." Kennedy got a piece of paper and his pen. "Tell me how to get to this camp, Hoagland, and I'll send those two on their way."

Jacob took the paper and pen and drew a quick map to the orchard. "Easy to find, if you follow this map, Constable. You'll go through this gully and watch the mud. It can be slick coming out."

The Hoagland's said goodbye and found their mounts. "Let's stop at the bakery on the way out of town, Son. A warm doughnut might taste pretty good right now. Looks like we'll be riding home in the rain, boy. You did all the right things this morning, Luke. I'm proud of you."

"So," Kennedy mused, "the small one's Slack Jaw Compton and the big one is Ted Upton. I'm gonna need some help on this." He struggled into his heavy coat and headed for Murphy's Inn and Tavern. "Two big strong men should be just fine." The cold air pushing heavy rain helped hurry the constable on the two-block walk. He mumbled to himself the entire way about mud, rain, snow, and two men who tried to burn his house down.

"Just in time for mid-day, Toby. The usual?" Murphy asked. "Have some fine roast pork today, or smoked elk. which one, Mate?"

"Just a belt of Ireland's finest, Murph. Looking for two strong men to help me roust a couple of beggars."

"Channing's logging crew were sent home early, Toby. They prefer cutting their timber in the sunshine, you know. They're in the dining room now. Might pick up a couple if you pay 'em."

"County offers four bits for helping me when I need it. That's a motivator, eh? Almost as much as I make." Kennedy took his whisky down and walked into the dining room. Five men were sitting at what Mrs. O'Reilly called the family table.

"Gentlemen," Kennedy said. "I could use two strong men, not afraid of a little tussle if it comes to that. Two men, you might know them, Ted Upton and Slack Jaw Compton are trespassing on Jacob Hoagland's place and I need to roust 'em out. Pays fifty cents and Murphy will throw in a drink, too." He took a glance over his shoulder hoping Murphy didn't hear him.

At the names, two of the men at the table make nasty noises and immediately said they would make the ride. "Won't be no need to be paying me to roust those two," Ned Walling said. "Lookin' forward to it."

"Same here," Grouchy Foster said. "Upton's a cheat, a swindler, and I'm gonna put welts on his head. Save your silver, Constable, but I will take the drink." Laughter rang out from the table and Kennedy told the two to meet him at his office in an hour.

"Bring a weapon, gentlemen. I'm told both men carry knives and probably have other weapons." He didn't mention anything about Upton and Compton being suspects in Judge Petrini's murder. *Get those two in separate cells and do some serious questioning and I might get the answers I'm looking for. I wonder which one's boot will match my drawings. The boot worn at the murder scene was the same type boot worn when they tried to burn my house down. And the same size.*

He was still furious that someone would try to burn him out. *Come to me face to face and we'll have it out but sneak around behind my back and burn my house down? You're a filthy swamp rat and I'll have you my way when I catch you.*

Kennedy had his double-barreled shotgun, a baton, and a knife ready to hand when Walling and Foster showed up. Each of them had a shotgun and knife as well. In the Oregon territory frontier of the late '40s, unless a man was hunting big game, the weapon of choice for protection was a shotgun and a knife. Kennedy outlined briefly where they were going and that he wanted both men to be brought back to Brookside alive.

"There are a few things they have to answer for, boys. These men are known to be dangerous, lads, but they know things that I need to know. they can't tell me those things if we kill the buggers."

"Gotta watch out for Upton, Constable. He's a shifty bloke and he'll stab you in the back first chance. Slack-jaw carries a big knife, but Upton uses a little dagger that does nasty work on a body," Walling said.

"I take it you've had a tussle or two with the man," Kennedy said. Walling just smiled as they headed for their horses.

"WHAT ARE WE GONNA TELL THE OLD MAN, TED? HE'S gonna be upset that Kennedy's house didn't burn." Slack-jaw Compton and Ted Upton were packing up their small camp, wanting to get out of the orchard after the surprise visit by the boy on a mule. "He wanted Kennedy to be frightened and back off his investigation of Petrini's death."

"Don't matter much to me what he says," Upton said. "We got paid. Let's ride toward Oregon City and make ourselves scarce around here. Sure as I'm talking to you, Kennedy recognized me when I ran last night. The old man can find someone else to do his dirty work."

"He paid us good, Ted and said there would be more coming. I think we should stick with him. Got ten dollars each and a bottle of rum and more coming, Ted."

Upton was a bruiser of a man, five feet nine at best but heavy from the waist up, with the broad shoulders of one who ran cross-cut buck saws in timber country. Unable to read or write, Upton got along by being the biggest, strongest, and meanest of the crews he worked with. His drinking was known far and wide in the industry. An ability to think his way out of a problem didn't exist.

"If we stay, we need a better place to set up a camp. Ain't neither one of us can go back to work, you know. Should have turned and knifed that constable instead of running. Won't run again, Slack-jaw. Should have slit him ear to ear and left him dead."

"Next time, Ted," Compton said. "Let's get out of here." Compton drove the buggy and followed the trail back down to the road to Brookside but turned west to come to and follow the river. It was a well-used trail and before they reached the little village they turned east. They would cross the main road south and continue into the foothills. "There's a creek up this way where we can set up camp. We can ride into town after dark and talk with the old man."

"Don't like that fat old man. Just sits around telling people what to do."

"He's got the money, Ted. Now, if we play our cards, we might have the money."

"What do you mean?" Upton asked, not under-standing at all what Compton hinted at.

"Have you been in his warehouse? The big one? Eh?"

Before Upton could answer Slack-jaw saw three riders coming down the main road out of town, the road they were about to cross. "Damn, it's Kennedy," he shouted, whipping the horse into a full gallop.

Kennedy spotted the carriage, saw the men trying to flee, and put the posse in a fast run after them. "There they are," he yelled. the chase was brief. The carriage horse wasn't up to a full out run uphill carrying the two men and their camp. Kennedy raced up alongside the carriage, aimed the shotgun at Slack-jaw and the man pulled the horse to a stop.

"Climb on down, you two and shuck your weapons. All of them." Kennedy said. Walling was on the other side of the carriage and when he stepped off his horse, Ted Upton made a lunge for him.

Upton was big, strong, and heavy, but a load of buckshot at less than three feet away stopped him cold. Walling stood stock still looking at the remains of the man he said he would put bruises on and felt weak. He'd never killed another human being, felt waves of nausea and turned to his horse.

"All right, Compton, you've seen what happens to a stupid man. Don't be one. Step down from the carriage, shuck those weapons of yours, and don't join your friend." *Typical of Upton. Damn fool. I've got to make sure we keep Compton alive. Have to know who killed the judge and who is masterminding the liquor fraud. Oh, and who tried to burn me out.*

Grouchy Foster stood behind Compton as he pulled a knife from his belt and dropped it. "Don't forget the other two," Foster said. Slack-jaw pulled one from his neck behind his head, and another from his boot. "You might want to strip him down, Constable. He's bound to have more."

"I will, Grouchy. Maybe walk him through town in his all-togethers. Tie him tight, Grouchy and let's get what remains of Upton in the carriage." He saw Walling struggling to get the body into the back of the carriage. "Here, lad, let me help there. You're about as white as a sheep."

"Ain'r never kilt nobody, Constable. Fought many, whipped most, but this is different. His head just exploded."

"Don't ever get used to it, Mr. Walling. Always see to it that it had to be done, and then don't do it again. Mr. Upton came at you with a knife and you did what had to be done. You were fully justified, Walling, and you better believe Upton would have killed you." Walling tried to smile, couldn't, and Kennedy watched him as he carefully tied the body in the carriage. *Probably killed dozens of deer without a thought, but this proves he's a good man, a decent man. Need more like him in Oregon.*

Kennedy had one prisoner, not two, and he hoped the one would have some answers for him. It's a fair bet, he thought, that Upton did the killing. *I'd bet another piece of silver that Slack-jaw set the fire, but neither one of those men have the brains to run the liquor fraud that might be at the base of all this. Or is it?*

It was a quick ride back to town with Walling driving the carriage and Grouchy riding alongside Kennedy. Kennedy's mind was churning its way through half a dozen different reasons for Judge Petrini to be dead. The liquor scheme was primary. Was there a challenge of leadership? Did Petrini take more than his share or did someone else? And what about his desire to be around young boys? Did some father take umbrage at that? There was always the possibility that it was none of the above, it might be something Kennedy knew nothing of as yet.

"Thank you, boys," the constable said, dropping Upton's body on Doctor Winslow's operating table. "I can handle things from here. Stop by the office for your silver and Murphy will see to it you're watered." He was chuckling to himself as the two lumbermen walked toward Murphy's.

"Certainly, made a mess of this fellow," the doctor said. "Cause of death is obvious to a blindman but I'll write you a report, Constable and have the body taken to Salinski. This close and he was shot with a scatter gun?"

"Attacked a man with a knife that close, Doctor. It could have been Ned Walling you'd be looking at.

Walling is lucky he has fast reflexes. Good men don't go looking to kill another, I'm sure you know, but there are times it must be done. Kill or be killed is the law of the frontier I'm afraid."

Kennedy drove the carriage with Slack-jaw Compton tied in the back to the county building. "All right, Compton, let's get you all comfortable in my little jail, eh?" He manhandled the tied up man out of the back and he fell to the ground. "On your feet, now." Compton didn't move and Kennedy poked him in the ribs with his boot only to hear some nasty words.

The constable didn't take kindly to some of the language being spewed about and grabbed the man by the ropes around his feet and dragged him through the dirt and up the stone stairway into the county building, down the hall and into his office. "Gentlemen don't talk that way in front of the ladies, Mr. Compton. I'll not have it."

He dragged the inert Slack-jaw into the lone cell at the back of the office, untied him and left, locking the iron door behind him. "We'll have a chat in a bit," he said. "Anyone you want notified that you're locked up? Or should I just hire a town crier to spread the news?" He tried and lost holding back his laughter and stoked the stove for some coffee. "Maybe just a dribble of some rum. eh?"

BROOKSIDE WAS A SMALL VILLAGE, A HUB, SURROUNDED BY farms and ranches. It didn't take long before the news of the death of Theodore Upton and arrest of Slack-jaw Compton was known by the majority of citizens. It was the viciousness of Upton's death that was spoken of most often. It wasn't long before Ned Walling found himself having to defend his actions.

Grouchy Foster was having a brandy in his coffee at the bar when he heard one of Upton's few friends start to berate Walling over the death. "You fired a shotgun in a man's face who was in arm's reach? You're just a killer. A real man would have simply knocked old Upton across the side of his head. No need to kill the man."

"You're wrong," Grouchy said, stepping between the two. "You weren't there so you didn't see the knife aimed at Ned's heart. You weren't there, Mr. Bigmouth, so you couldn't feel the terror of a man with a knife leaping from a carriage to kill you. Keep your filthy mouth shut about something of which you know nothing."

The man slammed his mug on the bar and turned to punch Grouchy when Murphy O'Reilly whacked him across the side of the head with a barrel bung. "That's enough." The logger fell to the floor but staggered back to his feet, the fight gone from him. "You've heard the truth from Grouchy Foster and from Ned Walling. Everyone knows Ted Upton would do what these men said he did, so let's not have any more about that here."

Similar scenes took place in other locations around Brookside, even in the comfortable aisles at the Ben Thorndyke store. "I've known the constable for many years," Ben said to a few men gathered around the pot belly stove near the candy counter. "If he's satisfied with how Upton's death took place, then I am too. Could it have been done differently? Possibly, but in the heat of the situation, a man leaping at you with a knife? Think about that before you think you'd do different."

Questions were raised and discussed, arguments were made and fisticuffs did happen, but after a day or two, it was accepted that Ned Walling had not over reacted. During that time, though, Constable Kennedy had little success in getting answers from Slack-jaw Compton.

Kennedy stopped in to see Claude Atkins. "Feeling better, Claude?"

"I am. Actually, moved about some this morning. Sybil says you captured the killers?"

"No, Claude. That's just talk around the village. Ted Upton and Slack-jaw Compton are suspects, but that's all, and of course, Upton's dead. Compton knows a lot more than he's willing to talk about, I'm sure. I've gone over everything I found at Petrini's home and in the judge's chambers and there's something I need to talk to you about if you are up to it."

"I'm looking forward to it," the county attorney said.

CHAPTER 22

"The judge wrote in his private diary about a conspiracy within the organization that imports and distributes the Virginia rum. I didn't find anything about that in your notes, however. Was it in his mind or was there a group moving to oust him?"

"That's something new to me, Toby. I was never able to get any real names, only the lower level workers not the men who managed the operation. Other than the judge, of course. He had to have help at high levels, Constable."

"I've seen Ed Creighton's name often, but he's been eliminated so who else with knowledge of how government works is in on this fraud? Another thing that bothers me, Claude. What if Petrini's death had nothing to do with the liquor scheme? What if I'm chasing a shadow instead of the real killer?"

"I've thought about that, too, but I'd stick with the fraud all the way. It's a criminal case even if it isn't the reason for the judge's death. It is possible you have two cases."

"Who in our little valley here would have knowledge

of how the territory's taxes are handled? Whoever is receiving that liquor has to pay a duty, a tax on it. The import duty is high, according to Murphy at the tavern. He gets some special stuff in from Europe and pays and pays for it, he says."

"To evade that duty would be intricate, Toby. I'm sure one or two of the county commissioners might know the process that must be followed and possibly be able to evade it. The county assessor would surely know, I would think, even though these are territorial taxes. I've not heard one of their names mentioned in any of my investigations."

Atkins took a deep breath before continuing. "Each barrel is marked, taxes paid and the date. Nothing leaves the docks or import warehouses without that mark. I'm sure Murphy will attest to this that territorial tax inspectors show up from time to time and those barrels better be marked." Kennedy nodded remembering Murphy saying such.

"I've got no jurisdiction out of this valley," Kennedy said. "If territorial officials are in the scheme, they're out of my reach. Any other names I don't know about?"

"Maybe not in your investigations, Claude, but County Commissioner Clyde Peabody was one of Petrini's drinking friends, and was close to Ed Creighton, as well." Kennedy had just a hint of a smile on his face as he got up to leave. "I'm going to bang Mr. Slack-jaw's head around some while I give a lot of thought to what we've just learned, Claude. Keep getting well," he said.

"WELL, SLACK-JAW, I SEE YOU'VE EATEN ALL YOUR MEAL today. That's good. It's easier to talk when you've had a good meal." Kennedy sat on a bench that ran along a solid stone wall inside the tiny cell and Slack-jaw Compton sat on an iron bunk with a straw mattress. "It would be a lot nicer if we had a mug of good Virginia rum, eh? Hard to get around these parts, though. So expensive."

Slack-jaw's eyes moved toward the constable, but he didn't say anything. Kennedy watched him move just a bit, maybe to get comfortable? Maybe squirming as Kennedy was too close to the truth. "Conversations are always better if more than one person is talking," Kennedy said. "Maybe I should ask old Clyde Peabody if he had a jug that we could have, eh?"

Compton's head jerked, he dropped his eyes, and Kennedy smiled slightly. *Thank you, Slack-jaw, you're not really being kind, though, are you?* "If I started asking, as I move about our fair little Brookside, would I find out that you, Ted Upton, and Clyde Peabody were known to be friends or acquaintances?"

"Don't know the man," Compton said. "Why are you holding me? I ain't done nothing. It was Upton tried to attack Walling, not me. I was driving the carriage. Ain't done nothing."

"You were trespassing on private property and threatened a little boy, Compton. Where were you last night, say, just after sunset?"

"Probably cooking some venison over an open fire," the man said. His broken jaw, inflicted years before had never been attended to by a doctor, never healed properly, and made for difficult talking. "Why?"

"Oh, just curious, Slack-jaw. Take your boots off, nice and slow, please." Kennedy watched as Compton unlaced the high timber worker's boots and left the cell. "You're sure you don't know Clyde Peabody?"

Compton didn't answer and Kennedy locked the cell and went into the office proper to measure the boot against what he measured at Petrini's and at his own home. *Perfect match. I'll get Upton's boots from Shorty and measure them, too. My money is on Compton being our killer.* He left the office and went up to the second floor to talk with court clerk Sven Olsen about Petrini's dealings with various county officials.

"THE MAN YOU WANT TO TALK TO, CONSTABLE, IS JOHN Henry Gutenberger." Kennedy was in Sven Olsen's office and Olsen was in a talkative mood. "He and Commissioner Peabody own Peabody-Gutenberger Drayage. They move merchandise all over the territory. Gutenberger runs the company and Peabody handles most of the paperwork end of things."

"Such as import taxes and such?" Kennedy asked.

"Yes, of course. The judge bought into the company recently and is now a one third partner. They have a large warehouse on the outskirts of Brookside, on the road to Oregon City."

"Were they needing money and Petrini bought in?"

"Partly, I think," Olsen said. "Ed Creighton was investing in the business, with the judge's help, and when he was murdered by his wife, the judge assumed Creighton's part."

Kennedy let the comment about murder go by, but not the rest of it. "You mean, Creighton's investment was simply transferred to Petrini?"

"It was all written and legal, I'm sure," Olsen said. "I'm sure I could find the documents if you think it's necessary."

"I do," Kennedy said. "It may help me find the judge's

killer." Kennedy watched for Olsen's reaction which came immediately.

"I'll get those papers right away, Toby. I'm sure they're in Petrini's private files here."

Private files? The first I've heard of this. I've been through the judge's chambers and office, even asked Olsen for all of Petrini's papers and there's been no mention of 'private files'. Another thought flashed through the constable's mind as he watched Olsen move a bookcase aside. Creighton was investing in this distributing company and his shares of ownership were transferred to the judge? Not to Irene Creighton?

He saw a conspiracy to sell illicit rum growing larger with every visit to Sven Olsen's office. He watched the bookcase move aside to reveal a cabinet built into the wall. *This is most interesting. Did Petrini have this built or someone way back in the 1830s when the courthouse was built? Are there other secret caverns in the old place?*

"Where does this Gutenberger live, Mr. Olsen? I'm sure it's not here in the valley."

"No, he travels down here from time to time, leaves the day-to-day operations to a warehouse manager named Smith, Terrence Smith. I'm sure you know that man."

Smith was a short, squat man of fifty or so years who was legendary in his consumption of beans, to the consternation of anyone who spent too much time around the man. "Yes, Sven, I do indeed. Do you know where this warehouse is? Oh, wait, it's the Butenberger warehouse. Smith is the manager" *That warehouse is plenty large enough to store many barrels of Virginia Rum. Right on the river with a dock as well.* Kennedy's mind was going at a fast pace and as long as Olsen was willing to answer questions, he would ask them.

Mr. Olsen seems to know everything there is to know about our dead judge. Is he involved? Is he part of the distribution scheme? If he were, why is he telling me all about it? There's something else I don't know anything about.

"Ah, here we are," Olsen said showing a sheaf of papers. There was a cabinet built into the wall that was hidden by a bookcase that could be rolled aside. Olsen closed the cabinet door and shoved the bookcase back. It moved into place easily. He turned and handed the papers to Kennedy.

The constable looked at the papers, Olsen, and the bookcase. *I wonder what else might be in that little cabinet? I wonder if anyone in the courthouse, besides our Mr. Olen knows about it? I wonder if I shouldn't make a little visit to these chambers some late night soon?* He couldn't turn his mind off, couldn't shut off the flow of questions.

"Thank you, Sven," Kennedy said and started to walk from the office. "Oh, that warehouse. Just where is it?"

"I don't think I know," Olsen said. "Judge always said on the outskirts of town. I've never been there. Must be somewhere in the valley, though."

What a strange little man, Kennedy thought walking back down to his office. *Knows the judge's personal business, his personal friends, thinks the old sot doesn't drink, but doesn't know where the judge's warehouse is. Or does he? It is after all the largest warehouse in Brookside that has a dock right on the river. Ben Thorndyke looks at it often, I'm sure.*

"Seems like I should set up shop here, Thorndyke," Kennedy said after Ben Thorndyke invited him into his private little log cabin office. "I've got another hundred or so questions for you, if you have time, that is."

"I will always have time for you, Toby. Sit and let's

talk. I might have some questions for you as well. Here, let me help you with that coat. It really will be spring soon."

Kennedy retrieved a sheaf of papers from the coat pocket and sat down in front of a hot fire. "Our fair minded and very dead judge was a businessman, Ben, and, it seems, in competition with you." Thorndyke's head swiveled up at the comment. "To a small degree, that is. Petrini, Clyde Peabody, and a man named John Henry Gutenberger own a company called Peabody-Gutenberger Drayage. You familiar with that?"

"Do they distribute rum that is not properly labeled, Constable?" Thorndyke chuckled.

"That is my next chore, sir. My money says yes, they do. Ed Creighton was an investor and when he died his shares went to Petrini for some odd reason I haven't figured out yet."

"Not to Irene and the children? Most odd." Thorndyke said. "You've obviously been busy, sir. Tell me more. I've heard the name Gutenberger. Something about a land scheme in Oregon City. I'll have to check on that. Peabody and Petrini distributing rum with a man known for land fraud. Hmmm."

"And, a land commissioner buying in?" Kennedy said. "One or more of the bunch found out that Petrini was holding out on them. That's what these papers are all about. Petrini's own set of books in which he details how he sells two barrels of rum but only reports to his fellow schemers that he sold one."

"Looks like you've found motive, Constable. Anything else?" Thorndyke reached into his desk and came up with a bottle of whiskey. "Shall we?"

Kennedy nodded with a smile. "Peabody's part in the business was his knowledge of how the territory taxes operate. Gutenberger had the distribution business, and the judge would have been protection, I believe, until Petrini got greedy. All in all, it was very profitable according to Petrini's own records. I need to have a long talk with Mrs. Creighton and see what she might know of her husband's dealings in the matter."

"If you come back here tomorrow morning at ten o'clock, you can talk with Mrs. Creighton in the comfort of my little office."

"And you'll be here, too? I would like that," Kennedy said.

CHAPTER 23

"Well now, Mr. Compton, it's time for us to have another fine chat," Constable Kennedy said, sitting down on the edge of the cot. "All this time I thought you were a logging man, working in Oregon Territory's primal forests and now I discover that no, you're a warehouse man, involved in the distribution of liquor around the territory. Why would I have been so wrong?"

Slack-jaw Compton sat down in the chair, opposite, and wouldn't look at Kennedy, wouldn't say a word. "Getting paid on a regular basis by County Commissioner Clyde Peabody, a gentleman you said you didn't know? Mr. Compton, really. Lying to me is a high crime punishable by a good thrashing, sir. Would you like to change your story, or would you prefer I bring my knotted and gnarled Irish walking stick in here?"

"I know him." Slack-jaw growled it out. "I move things for him sometimes and he pays me. He said he didn't want people to know."

"I'm one of those people," Kennedy chuckled. "Anything else you did for him?"

"Just an odd job from time to time."

"And Ted Upton? He worked for him as well?" Kennedy asked.

"No, Upton didn't work for him. Never did," Compton said. He squirmed about some and would not look the constable in the eye.

"But you were together the night my house was attacked. Come now, Mr. Compton, that walking stick is just a step or two from here. You and Upton tried to set my house afire. I saw you." He uttered that last phrase slow and loud and enjoyed watching Compton shrink from him. He reached out and jerked the man to his feet, pushed him out of the cell and into his little office.

"I'll need that answer, sir," Kennedy said, picking up his walking stick.

"Peabody paid for another man for some of these jobs but didn't know who I would pick."

Thank you again, Mr. Compton. So, Peabody paid you and another man to burn my house down, eh? He did that, why? Because I know too much about the Petrini case? Or because I know too much about the liquor fraud? Or, is there more? Kennedy's mind was spinning out of control, and he couldn't hide the smile on his face. *I wonder how many others get paid to do these little odd jobs of our fine county commissioner.*

"I have a very important meeting, Mr. Compton. I'll be back after and we'll continue our little conversation." Compton wasn't a man with a quick mind and wondered why the constable was smiling as he was ushered back into his cell.

It was a warm early spring morning that Kennedy walked through on his way to Thorndyke's office and a meeting with Irene Creighton. He was still enjoying the idea that he might be just hours from arresting someone for the murder of Judge Anthony Petrini. *Compton said Peabody hired him and another man to burn me out. It has to be because of what I know about Petrini. I wonder if he knows that I know about all the other things he's involved in?*

He knew he had to confront Commissioner Peabody soon, had to place the man under arrest but the only concrete thing he had was what Compton told him. "Evidence," he muttered. Without something in hand, the man might wiggle his way out of prison.

Another thought had been building, as well. Were there other county officials in on the liquor scheme? Were there other schemes, such as land fraud, involved? *Thorndyke said*

Gutenberger was involved in land fraud in Oregon City, is that why Creighton was brought in? "My God, but I'm full of it this morning," he said right out.

"Ah, Constable, come in," Ben Thorndyke said. "You know Mrs. Creighton, of course."

"Indeed," Kennedy said. "Good morning. You look well." He smiled at the lady, turned to Thorndyke and nodded before sitting down near the fire. "I've learned a couple of things since the death of Judge Petrini that I think we need to talk about, Mrs. Creighton. Will you stay, Ben?"

Ben Thorndyke nodded and sat behind his desk. Mrs. Creighton was in a chair near the fire as well. "Was your late husband a friend of County Commissioner Peabody, Mrs. Creighton?"

"I believe they knew each other. Something to do with land tracts that would be open for direct purchase rather than through the land commission. Mr. Creighton rarely discussed his businesses with me, but I did over-hear a few things from time-to-time."

Land tracts opening up for purchase? That's a new one.

Kennedy smiled. "Does the name John Gutenberger mean anything?"

"I've heard the name. Something to do with the land business, I think," Irene said. "Is this leading somewhere, Constable? Was Ed involved in something, um, improper?"

Kennedy smiled, nodded gently, and stood up. "Improper? Possibly. Illegal? Probably. Have you heard of a company called Gutenberger-Peabody Drayage?"

"Those names again, but as a company? No, I don't believe I have." Irene was frustrated at the questions that didn't seem to have any relation to her. "Please, Constable, can you come to the point?"

"I'm working hard to get there, Mrs. Creighton. It's come to my attention that Ed Creighton was investing money in that distribution company. Are you aware of that?"

"Investing? Money? Where would he get extra money to invest? As land commissioner he was paid a pittance, sir. No, I've not heard of such a thing."

Kennedy continued pacing around the small office building and finally sat back down. "It gets worse, I'm afraid, Mrs. Creighton. It seems every time we meet, I bring ugly news your way. My information shows that Mr. Creighton invested a fair sum and, following his death, the shares of the company that he owned were transferred to Judge Anthony Petrini."

Irene Creighton sat absolutely still, slowly moving her eyes back and forth from Constable Kennedy to Ben Thorndyke. "I don't understand," she mumbled. "He couldn't possibly have had enough money to invest in a company. Not telling me would be his way, but where would he have gotten that money?" The fact the shares were not transferred to her and the children didn't even enter her thinking. That, too, would be Creighton's way.

"And you knew none of this?" Ben Thorndyke asked. "Thank all the gods," he said.

"Why?" She looked amazed at his reaction. "Everything I learn about that man doesn't surprise me anymore. But having enough money to invest in a company? That does. We were always short of money, Constable."

"The point, my dear Mrs. Creighton, is that if you knew about all this you would probably have been a suspect in the murder of Judge Petrini," Thorndyke said. "Blessed good news," he said.

The silence held for many long seconds before Tobias Kennedy finally spoke. "I'm afraid Ben's right, and I'm glad you're not a suspect. Where the money Ed Creighton invested came from will have to be investigated, and why the shares of ownership in the company were transferred to the judge instead of to you and the children will also have to be investigated."

He stood up again and stared into the fireplace. "Have you discovered any papers, notes, or information that might be helpful, Mrs. Creighton? Right now, it appears that your late husband may have been involved in some illegal activities dealing with his land commission work. May I come over and go through his desk and office? It is important."

"I think that's a very good idea," Irene said. "I've not gone through anything. It's right now as it was the day he died and you would be most welcome to get it out of my house."

The arrangements were made and Kennedy said his thanks and headed out the door. Irene looked at Ben Thorndyke and tears rolled down her cheeks. "My husband, the father of my children was a criminal? I can't take much more of this. My son is involved, too? How much more am I to learn about that horrid man?"

"Kennedy is a superb investigator, Mrs. Creighton, so I believe we will all learn a lot in the coming days." He motioned for her to sit back down. "We'll put that aside and talk about my business, eh? I want to thank you for setting up this bookkeeping procedure of yours. Everything seems to make sense to me for the first time in years."

"It's rather simple, really, Mr. Thorndyke. It's a case of money out and money in." She smiled. "As long as the paperwork flows in, the books will always balance. It's when someone fails to send the proper paperwork that things get out of balance."

"You've made that very clear to me. I was one of those who thought he could remember every transaction, forgot to fill out bills or receipts, and fouled the books." He laughed and stoked the fire. "You've taught us all a good lesson in how to run a business."

Thorndyke got contemplative for a moment, looking at Irene. "You told the constable that you were always short of money when Creighton was alive." She nodded and he continued. "The office he held as land commissioner paid a fair wage, I believe, yet you called it a pittance."

"It was," she said. "What do you call a fair wage, sir?"

"My lead men receive thirty-five cents a day. What do you call that?"

"I believe that's fair, but, you see, Creighton only got twelve cents a day for all the work he did seeing to it that people were able to file on land."

Ben Thorndyke's eyebrows showed his reaction to what Irene said. He shook his head a couple of times, looked questioningly at her. "According to government orders, the land commissioner is to receive between thirty-five cents and fifty cents per day based on size of the territory and experience. Ed Creighton was closer to the fifty cents per day figure than the lower."

Irene sat still for several moments and Thorndyke saw the tears again tumbling down her cheeks and offered a hanky. "Such a foul example of a man," she mumbled. "We never really ate proper, yet he always had enough to drink with his chums. It was always my fault that we were short of silver in the tin box. I'm sorry, Mr. Thorndyke. this was my problem, not yours. I shouldn't be carrying on like this."

He sat back behind his desk and closed one of the ledgers she had brought in and smiled. "You said you've not done it, but I believe it would do you wonders to go through Creighton's effects. Why not go home, Mrs. Creighton, and you and Carrie spend the day knowing more about your late husband. You have every right and once Kennedy gets those papers you'll never have the opportunity."

It was a fearful thought, it was a wonderful idea, and Irene beamed as she slipped into her coat and headed for home. She and Carrie stopped at the bakery for some sweets to go with what she was calling a scavenger hunt. *It won't be as much fun as the real thing but on the other hand I might learn a lot about that terrible man.*

CHAPTER 24

"I'm becoming quite the pest, eh?" Tobias Kennedy said when Sybil Atkins opened the door. "Would it be possible to talk for just a couple of minutes with the county attorney?"

"He was hoping you might drop by, Constable, He's feeling much better today, come in."

"Claude, it's good to see you out of bed. Have time for a quick chat? I've learned much since our last visit."

"Good, Toby. That's good. I've got brandy in my coffee, would you like some?"

"Without the coffee, please," he said, giving Sybil a big smile. Claude Atkins was in an overstuffed armchair near the blazing fire and Kennedy sat in an adjacent chair. "We have a fine conspiracy among some interesting people, Claude. Commissioner Peabody is in the distribution business with John Gutenberger, Ed Creighton, and Anthony Petrini as partners."

"Oh, my," Atkins said. "Gutenberger? He's under investigation for land fraud by the territory attorney's office. Creighton? But, he's dead."

"Yes, all that, Claude. Creighton's share of the

company was transferred to Petrini on his death, not Mrs. Creighton or the children. Here's the part you'll like. Creighton was working with Gutenberger to free up land, not for distribution under the territorial plan but to sell to individuals."

"This is amazing, Toby. Just how many crimes are you investigating out of the judge's death?"

Kennedy laughed and took his snifter of brandy from Sybil. "Many of our fine citizens are going to be spending time in the territorial prison, I'm afraid." He took a long drink of brandy and smiled. "Good brandy, Claude. Oregon made, is it?"

"'Tis indeed, sir. When do you plan to make some arrests? I'll need to be ready to prosecute. Have you any of this in writing? With what you've told me, I'll need to bring some young bucks down from Oregon City to help. Give those fine young attorneys a taste of real crime, eh?"

"You'll have a full summary of where I am by tomorrow. Petrini was killed for holding out on the other partners, I'm certain. I believe Commissioner Peabody hired the killing done and I'm holding that man now. When I have his full confession, I'll arrest Peabody."

"That's wonderful. And all the rest will just fit into place, eh?" Atkins was smiling and got to his feet. "I'm feeling much better now. Where did this all come from?"

"Mostly from Sven Olsen, the judge's clerk. Seems he knows just about everything there is to know about Petrini."

"He wanted to go to work for me before he ended up with the judge. His father and grandfather were tree fellers and he wanted to be one, too. Boy didn't have it in him, though. Never grew big and strong despite his trying. He'd show up on the job, new boots and all, but didn't have the strength. The other men weren't kind to him, either."

"Interesting," Kennedy said. "Well, back to the office. I have a lot of writing to do. Thank you for the brandy."

It was a good walk back on a fine late spring day. *So, Olsen wanted to be a logger, eh? Somehow, he's the key to many questions, most importantly that hidden wall cabinet. I might have to take a walk upstairs later this evening.*

Irene and Carrie were in Ed Creighton's little office just off the main room of their home. There were two file cabinets, a desk, a wall library, and two chairs in front of the desk and one behind. Irene wiped off the top of the desk, dusty since no one had been in the room since his death. The desktop was empty as Irene took the chair behind the desk.

"This probably isn't going to be fun, Carrie, and if you'd rather be upstairs reading, I'll understand." She noticed, not for the first time how much Carrie had grown in the time since Creighton's death. Matured, maybe, more than grown, although the girl was taller. *She's so much like I was at that age. Interested in everything, needed to know answers to questions most adults couldn't even ask, and loved books.*

"I think I'd like to stay, Mama. Papa would never let me in here. He used to invite Jeremy in and would tell me to go away, this was a man's room. He slammed the door in my face once. It really hurt."

Irene reached out and grabbed her daughter, hugged her as close as she could, and cried, softly, squeezing Carrie to the point the girl had to try to get loose. "I'm sorry, honey. I think we both needed that hug. This room is part of our home, and it will be turned into our sewing room when all this is taken out. So, where should we start? The desk?"

She started with the center drawer, pulled everything out and laid it on the desktop. A small ledger caught her eye immediately as it was marked "Personal". *I remember having to teach that foul man how to keep his books. Had no natural closeness with numbers or the rationale behind keeping one's books.*

After more than an hour Irene stood up and found Carrie engrossed in a book about shipbuilding in New England. "Where did that come from?"

"Gerald Thorndyke gave it to me. It's what he wants to do, only here in Oregon Territory, not back east. I'm hungry, Mama."

Irene was amazed at the time when they walked into the kitchen. "We squandered most of this day, eh?" She said. They had some biscuits and jam and a piece of cake, and Carrie went upstairs to read some more while Irene slipped back into Creighton's office and that ledger.

If these numbers are even halfway correct, there is a lot of our money floating around out there, somewhere. She caught herself, realizing she was thinking 'our' money, not his. *It always should have been our money but was always his.*

It appeared from the books that a rather large amount of money was kept in a box somewhere in the house. Other money was in a bank account in Oregon City, and a considerable amount had been invested in the Peabody-Gutenberger Drayage company.

She wanted to lay her head on the desk and cry for an hour or more and knew she couldn't. "The laws of the territory are against me," she whimpered, then sat straight up and said in a strong voice, "No, I won't simply give it up."

As a woman she would be fighting a definite uphill

battle to claim what Creighton had, and the fact she had killed him, gave the other side even more power. *I need an attorney and the problem there is, the attorney would be a man.* Interesting that since she wasn't aware that quite a bit of the money came from illegal activities, she would not have known that it wouldn't have been hers anyway.

At supper, Irene and Carrie talked about what had been found. Irene tried to let Carrie know that they might have some things coming to them, but it would be a fight to get them. How do you tell an eight year old how dreadfully women are treated by most men.

It was after supper that Irene said, "Let's have some fun. Somewhere in this house your father has hidden a wooden box. I'm sure it would have a hinged lid and a big lock of some kind. We'll start in that office and then go room-to-room until we find it." She made it a game and Carrie was the one who should get the prize.

"Jeremy has a locked box under his bed, Mama. I saw him take it out once in a while and then sneak it back. He never knew that I saw him."

Irene's heart almost stopped, and she sat back down quickly. "Can you bring it down here, honey? There was a single key on a string in your father's desk that I'll bet you a sugar coated doughnut will open that box."

Carrie giggled and ran upstairs. She came back with a box that measured about ten inches square and maybe six inches deep. "It's heavy, Mama," she said, setting it on the table. "I almost dropped it."

"I should have gotten it, honey. I wasn't thinking. Let's see what we can find, eh? What do you think is inside this box?"

"Jeremy always had a pocket full of marbles. But that would be a lot of marbles," Carrie said, and Irene had to laugh.

"The box was your father's, not Jeremy's," she said. She inserted the key into the lock with ease, turned it, and grasped the latch to open the box. *I wish Mr. Thorndyke was here, somebody I could trust. If this box is full of silver I'm going to faint, I know it.* She lifted the lid and gasped, clutching at her throat. The lid fell back into place and Irene sat stock still, her fingers still at her throat.

CHAPTER 25

"My heavens. Mrs. Creighton. Are you ill?" Beverly Thorndyke answered the heavy pounding at the front door of their home. "Come in, dear, come in. I'll get Ben." Irene sat heavily at a small couch near the fire, holding the heavy box in both hands. Carrie sat next to her.

"My goodness, you're white as a sheet, Mrs. Creighton," Ben Thorndyke said. "Let me get you a brandy. What is it that brings you to my home this late in the evening."

She tried to shake off the brandy but Ben insisted she take at least a small taste. "I'm embarrassed at just showing up this late, Mr. Thorndyke, but I didn't know who else to talk to. Here," She said, "open this and you'll understand. Then I have a small ledger you must see."

Ben Thorndyke took the box to an end table and opened the latch. She heard him take a quick and deep breath when he lifted the lid. "Where on earth did you find this?" He left the box on the table and sat down across from Irene. "There must be several hundred dollars worth of gold coins in that box."

"It was Mr. Creighton's," she said. "Look through this, if you would, please." She handed him the small ledger.

Thorndyke spent several minutes going through the pages of figures. "Does Constable Kennedy know about all this?" Irene shook her head. "Creighton has considerable money in an Oregon City bank? Has this box of several hundred dollars? Some of it must be from his wages, surely, but definitely not all of it. Kennedy talked about possible land fraud, liquor tax fraud, and a distributing company. Ed Creighton's part in that would not bring in this much money."

Thorndyke hollered out for his eldest son, Peter, to run and find Constable Kennedy, that it was imperative for the man to come immediately. "You've done the right thing, Mrs. Creighton. Some of this must be legitimate, but you realize that most of it is from illicit activities."

I'm afraid I do," Irene whimpered. *Despite being dead that man has found yet another way in which to hurt me and his family.*

"GOOD HEAVENS, BEN, WHAT IS IT THAT YOU'VE SENT YOUR son to fetch me? It's nigh on to ten o'clock, sir."

Thorndyke laughed as the disheveled constable was rushed into the living room. "I'll fix you a brandy, get yourself settled, sir, and then you'll have reason to be upset." Kennedy slipped out of his coat while Ben filled a snifter with brandy. "I'll let Mrs. Creighton explain why you've been called."

It was more than an hour later that Kennedy left the Thorndyke home carrying a small ledger and a heavy wooden box, locked tight. *A night I'll not soon forget. First that hidden cabinet and now a box full of gold coins.* He got a lamp lit in his office and for the second time that night, opened the safe.

Kennedy had just returned to his home from the courthouse, earlier, when young Thorndyke fetched him. What he found in the cabinet in the judge's chambers astounded him and frightened him. Inside that hidden cabinet were the working books of the entire conspiracy. Names, dates, and amounts, all in a hand he didn't recognize. Those items went in the constable's office safe.

As Brookside Constable, Kennedy was familiar with the penmanship of County Attorney Atkins and Territorial Judge Anthony Petrini. He didn't recognize whoever did the writing in the company records. Now, he has another set of financial records, but in Ed Creighton's hand along with a box full of gold. What he saw was a double conspiracy and it probably led to the judge's murder. People within the initial fraud were scheming to steal from their partners and getting caught.

Now, my fine friend, I have to put names to all these transactions. Who is the man stealing from the company? I was sure it was Petrini and that led to his death, but after reading all those pages of numbers I'm not so sure. The thefts from the company led to Petrini's death, that I'm sure. But I'm equally sure, now, that it wasn't Petrini doing the thieving. There's someone else involved.

"I'll get this all figured out after the sun comes up," he muttered. "Time to go home and sleep on it."

Early spring in the rolling foothills country along Oregon's Willamette Valley was wondrous, green, and wet. All of that as Kennedy walked from his home to the courthouse, which he found in a scene of bedlam.

"What is it?" He asked one of the clerks.

"Oh, Constable, it's Commissioner Peabody, dead, sir. Stabbed and dead." The young clerk, a man named Stark, was shaking in fear and pointed toward the county commissioner's office, just steps from Kennedy's. The constable hurried to the scene, moved several people out of the way, and found Doctor Winslow hovering around the body.

"Glad you're here, Kennedy. Nasty stuff, these murders. Here, look at this," Winslow said. Kennedy saw slashes across the chest and abdomen of Commissioner Peabody, through his vest and shirt and deep into flesh and internal organs. "Opened the man right up, and then stabbed at the vitals."

"Didn't leave us the weapon, either, eh?" Kennedy said. "What else have you found?"

Winslow knelt down to point out something and Kennedy joined him. "Your killer isn't large and strong, Constable, but fast. I think Peabody may have fought off the initial attack but when the killer started slashing back and forth, he was overwhelmed. That knife is as sharp as some of my tools."

"Who found this and when?" Kennedy asked.

"I guess I did," the clerk Stark said. "When I first opened the courthouse. It was near seven, I think."

"You say you opened the courthouse? The doors were locked?" Kennedy knew that he had locked up when he left. When did Peabody arrive?"

"No, the doors were already unlocked and that surprised me," Stark said. "That's when I started going from office to office to see if someone was here and found poor Mr. Peabody." Stark was still shaking from the experience, but Kennedy knew he had to continue the questioning. If he stopped, the man might forget something important.

"Did you find anyone else?"

"No, but I'm sure I heard someone walking around in the offices upstairs. I didn't go up, I ran to get the doctor."

Kennedy ushered everyone out of Peabody's office, told Stark not to let anyone in, and walked quickly up the stairs. *Stark isn't the killer. My killer will be covered in Peabody's blood.* The second floor held court clerk Olsen's office and the chambers and courtroom of Anthony Petrini. There was a storeroom for court supplies and a holding cell for those who were rowdy in the courtroom as well. Kennedy roamed through the various rooms and didn't find anyone nor anything that seemed out of place.

It was just a hunch that made him walk back into the judge's chambers. He pushed aside the bookcase and found the door to the secret cabinet open. *Well, well. I'm positive I closed and latched that little door.* Kennedy looked inside and found it empty. "I only took what I thought was evidence," he muttered. "Most interesting."

The wall clock showed it was well after ten o'clock and Kennedy walked back down to the main level. Courthouse personnel, people looking to do business with the courthouse, and a few people who arrived after hearing of Peabody's murder. "Anyone seen Sven Olsen?" Kennedy asked.

"He left as soon as I brought Doctor Winslow," Stark said. "He was crying, almost retching, sir."

Kennedy mumbled something and slipped into his office. *Isn't this interesting. Well, at least I think I know who might have been upstairs.* He knelt in front of his office safe to see just what had been done. "Tried to break the dial right off the machine," he muttered. "Stronger than I thought it was." Whatever tools had been used were gone.

Kennedy tried to put it together. Did Olsen arrive early and discover someone had been in the secret cabinet and decide it was Kennedy? Did he then come downstairs to break into Kennedy's safe and was interrupted by Commissioner Peabody? Or was it Peabody who was trying to break into the constable's safe? Olsen arrived early, and a fight took place?

I've far too many questions and nary enough answers. There is a considerable amount of money involved and the leading characters are dying off quickly. Who is gaining the most from those who have died? The only partner left alive, John Gutenberger who lives far away in Oregon City. Ah, but a certain Terrence Smith is his warehouse manager here in Brookside. I wonder what he would know about all this?

Kennedy wiped his brow, muttering about overthinking the situation when Doctor Winslow stuck his head in the doorway. "I'll have the report over to you as soon as I can, Constable. Is this connected in any way to Petrini's death?"

"That is yet to be determined, Doctor," Kennedy said. He wasn't going to give the man anything else to talk about at Murphy's. "Thank you. Did it look to you like someone may have tried to clean up some?"

"You mean from blood flowing like the Missouri? I had that feeling, yes."

Kennedy walked to Peabody's office and found Stark keeping people out. "Thank you, Stark. Tell me what you heard while I look over the scene in here."

"All I heard was someone walking around."

"Walking or running? Hurrying?"

"I was horrified at finding Peabody, Constable, and knew I had to get the doctor. I remember hearing what sounded like someone walking around upstairs. That's all." Stark was again shaking in fear and Kennedy sent him out of the bloody office.

Like Petrini's killer, whoever did this had to be splashed with a lot of blood. I know Olsen was upstairs when Stark brought the doctor back, but was he upstairs when the killer hit? Or is Olsen the killer? He couldn't find any bloody footprints, no sign of someone dripping blood while leaving the office. *I think it's time for a visit with Murphy O'Reilly. I need an hour all to myself to put this together. Then I'll need to track Sven Olsen down. Ah, and I mustn't forget Mr. Smith at the Gutenberger warehouse. It's not logical for the senior partner to eliminate his partners in this way. The arrow points solidly at Gutenberger being behind the murders, but is he really stupid enough to think that it wouldn't? I must keep him in mind but only as a side thought.*

Kennedy kept thinking there was someone else, someone whose gain might not be what most would consider wealth. Maybe position? Power? Authority?

CHAPTER 26

S pring was making itself known throughout the little valley. There were warm days filled with bright sunshine, which brought more and more greenery out each day, and farmers were busy making their ground ready for planting. Spring on a frontier farm in the magnificent Oregon Territory was a busy and difficult time. Cattle were giving birth, and flocks of sheep seemed to grow in size overnight. Brookside, too, showed more and more signs of the bringing forth season as some residents were found working in their kitchen gardens and planting flowers.

Mud was the dominant feature of farms, ranches, pathways, walkways, and roads. One didn't venture outdoors without first being ready to face the mud. On everyone's tongue was the phrase, "It'll dry out soon enough." Plows were covered, horses and mules legs were covered, and even the boardwalks along the main thoroughfares were splashed with the stuff.

Constable Tobias Kennedy didn't see much of that as he made the two block walk to Murphy's tavern.

Sunshine splashed his ruddy face but there was no sign of a smile. *I need to visit that warehouse and have a chat with the manager, Terrence Smith, and I need to know the whereabouts of one John Henry Gutenberger. All of that after I find Sven Olsen. What a mess.*

"People are starting to talk, Tobias," Murphy said when the constable arrived.

"About what, exactly, Murph?"

"About people being killed, you dolt. First the judge, now a county commissioner. Is there a murderer running amok in our fair valley? That's the question being asked. Don't spit a chunk of blarney at me, Toby. I'm asking too."

"Ah, well then, I'll tell you that the little people are out in force killing, pillaging, and raping the countryside. There, Murph, is what I know at this time. How about a wee touch of the old country in a clean glass, now?"

"I'd like to be helpful," Murph said. "With that attitude you'll not get much help."

"I'm sorry, Murph. I know you want to help. I need some help, too." He wanted to tell his long time friend everything, the box of money, the files filled with illegal transactions, the ideas he had about the two killings, and knew it would be spread through town in an instant.

"Does Sven Olsen drink in this fine establishment, Murph?"

"I've seen him have a bite of Mrs. O'Reilly's fine food, but I don't believe the man is much of a drinker. Not much of a man, either."

"Oh? And just what does that mean?" Kennedy asked.

"Wanted to fell trees but didn't have the strength to swing an ax, Toby. Men called him Baby-boy on the job. He's a coward, too. Never would fight back. As court clerk he's got the judge's protection. He worships that judge."

"Might worship him but doesn't know the first thing about the man. Swears Petrini never took a drop of booze. Do you know where I might find Terrence Smith?"

"At the Gutenberger warehouse. North of town on the river. Has its own dock. Big red building. What do you want with that smelly rat?"

"Hopefully, some answers," Kennedy said. The draught of fine Irish whisky went down fast, and Kennedy was again on the prowl.

"WELL, SON, WE'VE HAD A GOOD SEVERAL DAYS. LET'S take a little time for ourselves, eh? How about a ride down to the river and see what spring looks like down there?"

Warm spring temperatures, irrigation ditches running full, and several days of plowing and seeding had Jacob Hoagland ready for a short break in the routine. "We'll plant the rest of our place in the next two days and then start on the new property."

It would be just a few short weeks and fields of corn, wheat, and barley would color the brown earth with many shades of green. Other fields were in beans, potatoes, onions, and garlic. "I need to pick up our new contracts with Gutenberger Drayage, Luke, so that will be our first stop, and the rest of our seed order is waiting for us at Thorndyke's."

"I bet they have fresh doughnuts at the bakery, Papa." Luke laughed when Jacob poked him in the ribs.

The team of mules was harnessed and hitched to the wagon, and they were off. Hoagland was teaching Luke the fine art of driving a team and the boy was doing well. For one as young as he was, starting his ninth year, holding two reins in each hand became natural in just a couple of lessons. "You'll be walking behind a plow soon, boy, and driving the seeder, too."

"Mama gave me a note and wants us to drop it off at Mrs. Creighton's. It would be nice to see Carrie again. She's a nice girl."

"Oh, is that so?" Jacob chuckled. The ride into town was quick and as they passed the courthouse Hoagland wondered about the large number of people who seemed to be gathered about. He made the turn onto River Road and followed it to the Gutenberger warehouse.

He tried his best to ignore the meandering stench that surrounded the man. "Morning, Mr. Smith. Looks like the river's got a good flow this spring."

"Does," Terrence Smith said. They were standing on the dock enjoying the sunshine. "I have your contracts all drawn up as you and Mr. Gutenberger wanted them. Got your planting done?"

"Almost, sir. Almost. Keep the rains away for another week and we'll be done." As they made their way into the large warehouse, Tobias Kennedy rode up and dismounted. "Good morning, Constable," Hoagland said.

"And to you sir. Hello Smith. I'm afraid I have some bad news for you. Mr. Peabody was killed this morning. You will need to get word to Mr. Gutenberger."

"My God, Constable," Smith said. He left it at that. Kennedy was surprised at the lack of reaction. Within a period of just a couple of months three of the four partners in the firm were dead, all victims of violence.

Smith turned to walk into his office. "What happened? Who did it?"

"Is that what the crowd in front of the courthouse was all about?" Jacob Hoagland asked.

"Yes," Kennedy said. "Man was knifed early this morning. Brutally murdered in his own office." Kennedy tried not to make it obvious but looked Smith up and down and couldn't see a spot of blood on his clothing or boots.

"Has Sven Olsen been by this morning, Smith?"

"No. Since the judge was killed, he rarely comes by. I get notes from him, as always, telling me what Mr. Gutenberger wants."

"Gutenberger tells Olsen who then tells you? I was under the impression you were the manager here." Smith didn't say anything, just turned his head aside. Kennedy tried to hold in his surprise at the comment.

Why wouldn't Gutenberger send his orders directly to Smith? Just how is Olsen connected to this fraud? His name doesn't appear on any of the documents, there are no payments directed his way. Kennedy pulled a handkerchief and wiped sweat from his brow.

"Mr. Smith, since before Christmas, this company has had three stockholders killed. Mr. Creighton, Judge Petrini, and now, Commissioner Peabody. What is Mr. Olsen's position in the organization? You're the ware-house manager and at this time, the sole owner appears to be John Henry Gutenberger. Where does Sven Olsen fit in?"

"All I know is I get my orders from Olsen. You want more? Talk to Olsen." Smith turned to his desk and found some papers. Kennedy felt he was edging close to some answers. Getting Smith upset, the man might spout something he shouldn't.

"These are the contracts that Mr. Gutenberger wants

from you, Mr. Hoagland." Smith was ignoring Kennedy and the constable did not like being ignored.

"Mr. Smith, I've not been rude to you, sir. Don't be rude to me. I asked simple questions and I want simple answers. What is Sven Olsen's position in this operation?"

He saw Smith tighten up, scowl at his desk. He was angry and more to the point, was embarrassed. "I got my orders from the judge through Olsen before the judge was killed. Now I get my orders from Gutenberger through Olsen. I have no more idea than you why. Why didn't the judge just come down and tell me? Why doesn't Gutenberger send me his requests hisself? Olsen's a petty little whelp who needs a good thrashing, if you want my opinion. That clear things up, Constable?"

Smith wasn't the kind of man who people would take advantage of. His size alone stopped most, and his attitude, which was generally of the angry sort, kept others at bay. It did not deter Constable Kennedy. "Not in the least, Mr. Smith but thank you for telling me this. Is Gutenberger expected?"

"Haven't seen the man in a year," Smith said. "He's far too busy with all those upstanding territorial nabobs in Oregon City to bother with the likes of me."

Kennedy had been pacing around the alcove of an office trying his best to see into the dark depths of the warehouse, looking for kegs or barrels of untaxed rum. If there was any, it was well hidden. "Thank you, Smith," he said, nodded to Hoagland, smiled at Lucas, and walked out of the warehouse.

"Interesting situation you're in, Mr. Smith. thank you for these contracts and let's hope I can overfill this old building." Jacob Hoagland and Luke walked to the wagon for the short ride to Thorndyke's emporium.

Kennedy waved them down and the two wagons moved along slowly, side by side. "Don't mean to pry, Mr. Hoagland, but exactly how do you get paid for your produce and meat?"

"I have commercial buyers in the territory, even some up north in Washington, and when they place their orders, I ship what they need. Their payments back to me show where Gutenberger takes his shipping fee out. Why?"

"Have you ever had a problem receiving your money? Does it come in cash, coin, or bank receipt?"

"Rather personal, Constable, but I will say that I've never had a problem. Gutenberger has always been fair and honest with me. Good day, sir," Hoagland said. He took the reins from Lucas and nudged the mules into a trot. *Interesting situation he's in. Dead people and no answers. I wonder how Peabody's seat will be filled. Can't run the county with two commissioners.*

"Constable Kennedy wasn't very nice," Lucas said.

"He's trying to find out who killed Judge Petrini and Commissioner Peabody, Son. He has to ask hard questions and I didn't want to answer them. It's none of his business and it has nothing to do with any of the murdered men how we get paid for our produce." Hoagland wondered why it would matter to Kennedy how he was paid.

Kennedy smiled at Hoagland's response but shook his head at not getting the information he wanted. He was hoping that the big farmer would say that it was delivered by Sven Olsen, or that the judge called him in and Olsen doled it out. *I don't know why but I'm sure that Olsen is the key to most of my questions.*

. . .

"Jacob, good morning," Ben Thorndyke hollered out when Hoagland brought the wagon up to Thorndyke's loading dock. "Got several hundred pounds of seed for you. How's your spring coming?"

"Rains have been timely, Ben, and the snow is melting right on schedule. Seems like it's been a bit dangerous to be living in Brookside, though. Just heard that Commissioner Peabody was killed this morning. What's bringing all this on?"

"Not sure, Jacob, but I believe it has to do with illegal liquor deals and some intrigue within those deals. Let's have some coffee while the boys load you up. Want a piece of hard candy, Lucas? Red or green?"

They stepped into the main farm supply building and ran into Irene Creighton bringing some papers for Thorndyke to sign. "Good morning, Mrs. Creighton. You look well," Jacob said. "I think Lucas has something for you."

"I do," Luke said. "Is Carrie with you?" He reached in his pocket and brought out the folded letter. "It's from mama."

"Thank you, Lucas. Carrie is with Gerald in the main office over there. Go over and say hello. She's asked about you." Irene opened the folded paper and read the note.

"This is awfully nice, Mr. Hoagland," she said. "Carrie and I would enjoy supper with all of you on Sunday. Let me write a quick note back." She hurried into the office and Jacob joined Ben Thorndyke for coffee.

"Nasty business, these killings," Ben said.

"Being out in the fields all day I don't get to hear much about the town's doings. How is it that the judge, a county commissioner, and the land agent are connected. You gave that impression."

"Seems they were partners with Mr. Gutenberger in his drayage business and possibly other enterprises, some of which might be illegal efforts. Constable Kennedy has his work cut out for him."

"Indeed," Jacob said. "Creighton was in a partnership with the judge? Maybe that's why some people got more favorable deals than others. More than one person got their land allotment by way of special offerings, bribes if you will."

What Hoagland said made Thorndyke think of the little wooden box filled with gold coins and the bottles of rum that Kennedy talked about. "Always thought of the man as a criminal, but never associated him with the judge or Commissioner Peabody until recently," Ben said. He didn't go any further, didn't mention that the Gutenberger bunch might have been selling land that was supposed to be given.

"Any idea how they'll fill the empty commissioner's seat?" Jacob Hoagland sipped his coffee.

"Well, Jacob, if I had any say in it, I'd appoint you. Actually, though I guess names will be offered and the two who are left will decide."

"Me? Why would you say something like that?"

"We had Peabody from the timber business and Conroy from the timber business, and old Mr. Dudley from the bank. I think we need a rancher's voice on the commission. think about, Hoagland. You'd be a natural."

Jacob looked the man in the eye and had to smile. *A natural? A terrified natural, maybe. I'm not much for telling people what to do or how to do it.* Hoagland shook his head and changed the subject. "How is Mrs. Creighton getting along?" Jacob asked. "She looks well."

"I and two of the lumber companies are keeping her busy, sir. She's a whiz at this keeping of the books. Because of her dead husband she will be facing problems as more and more of his life comes to light, though. She's a tough one." He laughed and poured more coffee. "My son, Gerald and her daughter, Carrie are best of friends, even to the point of planning a business together."

"A business? At their age?" Jacob snickered and then thought about it. After all, wasn't he teaching Lucas to be a farmer and rancher? Wasn't Lucas already planning his future? "What kind of business would that be, Ben?"

"Seems Gerald has been studying the engineering of ship building and believes the future of sea transport is the same as what they are seeing in the east with these incredible steam machines. Ten years old and he's catching the ears of some in the industry. I'll stick to my mules for the time being," Ben laughed.

Hoagland's mind was going in circles. Gerald Thorndyke was ten, Lucas was almost nine, and Carrie Creighton was eight-years-old, and each was in their own way, working on their future. "I think this old world of ours will be just fine in the future, Ben, with children like ours at the helm, so to speak."

"Ha!" Ben snorted. "Right you are, Jacob. We might be leaving them a mess but they're on the right road."

Jacob signed for his seed, gathered up Lucas, and they headed back for the farm. "You and Carrie have a good time?"

"I like her, Papa, but so does Gerald. He's pretty smart, too. He built a boat out of small sticks but it doesn't have any masts or sails. He says it runs on steam. I don't think he knows what he's doing."

Jacob had to chuckle. "I've heard about these steam engines, son. They're real." The rest of the ride home

involved discussions of plowing, seeding, and watering
the new one hundred acres and the visit on Sunday by
the Creighton ladies. There was no mention of a seat on
the county commission, but the thought did rumble
around Jacob Hoagland's heads for the entire trip. *I
wonder what Martha will say about this?*

CHAPTER 27

Constable Kennedy walked down the muddy Third Avenue to a small wooden cabin with a cedar shake roof and sturdy rock chimney. Number Twelve, Third Avenue, Brookside belonged to Sven Olsen but despite his pounding Kennedy was not going to be talking to the owner. "No smoke from the fireplace, no answer to my pounding, no tracks after the fresh rain, and I wonder where Mr. Olsen might be?"

The muttering continued as Kennedy walked around the small building, checked the carriage house, the enclosed back yard, filled with weeds, but no garden, and tried to look into a couple of the curtained windows. "No one has been into or out of this house since it rained yesterday afternoon," he said. He wrote a quick note and tucked it in the crack between door and jam and headed back to Main Street with its boardwalk, getting him out of the mud.

"Murphy, I need another man or two. Anybody in that back room of yours we can trust? Maybe Ned Walling?"

"Walling's in the back having his stew, Toby. You eating or drinking?"

"Both," Kennedy laughed. "After I talk with Walling. Set 'em up, Murph. I'll be right back." He walked into the back room and found Walling at the family table, the remains of a hearty meal in front of him.

"Open for a little more work with me, Mr. Walling?" Kennedy asked. "No danger to speak of this time around."

"It wasn't the danger that bothered me, Constable. It was the killin'." He took a swipe at his mouth with a napkin and stood up. "What's on your mind?"

"I can't seem to find our fine court clerk, Sven Olsen. He hasn't been home, but his mule and cart are home. It'll be four bits a day if you can find the man for me. Don't try to arrest him or even hold him, just tell me where he is. Don't want to frighten the man into doing something stupid or running away."

"I understand," the lumberjack said. "Beats working in the mud all day. He won't be looking to shoot me, will he?" Walling still had bad dreams of Upton leaping at him with a knife.

"No, I don't believe so," Kennedy chuckled. He headed back to the barroom and found his table set, a bowl of lamb stew steaming nicely, and a bottle of Ireland's finest next to a clean glass.

"Are you trying to impress me? Or bribe me for something, Murphy?"

"No bribe, Toby. Mrs. O'Reilly is afraid and I want you to tell me that she has no reason to be so."

"Afraid because of the recent killings? She has no reason to be afraid, sir. These were men involved in criminal activity fighting amongst themselves for power and wealth. Her kitchen and pantry are as safe as ever."

"She'll be thankful to you, Toby, as I am."

The meal certainly tasted as good as it smelled, but all of that was lost to the constable as his mind worked its way through the fact that three of the four owners of a business were dead and the fourth was far off in Oregon City. "Not a soul to brace," he murmured.

He couldn't help remembering that he was sure that Commissioner Peabody had hired Slack Jaw Compton and Theodore Upton to kill the judge and set fire to his house, so who then hired whom to kill Peabody?

"Or are the two killings not even related?" He said it right out and had to look around to make sure no one was paying attention. *That would put a bug in the soup wouldn't it? I'll set that thought aside for the time being. It's a mess with all my focus on Sven Olsen only because he's the only one of the bunch left alive in our fair village.* He had to chuckle at the thought.

"You seem to be enjoying yourself, Constable," Ben Thorndyke said. He pulled out a chair. "Mind some company? This Peabody killing has our Brookside worked up. Any ideas on who or why?"

"Ideas only, I'm afraid, Ben. As we talked earlier, I was ready to arrest Mr. Peabody for what I believed was his part in the murder of Judge Petrini. It's sticky, Ben. Four partners in an illegal liquor scheme and three of them dead in just a few months. I was told today that Mr. Smith at Gutenberger's warehouse gets his marching orders from Sven Olsen who isn't even listed as a Gutenberger employee more or less a stockholder in the company."

"Most interesting. That man is a worm, Constable."

"Oh? In what way?" *Almost the same words Claud Atkins and Smith used to describe the man. I've just considered him one who might be called a brown-noser the way he was always with Petrini.*

"He was run off by the lumberjacks who work for Claude Atkins and came sniveling to me for work. He implied that he could do this and that, probably better than the men who already worked for me. I've seen his kind before, Toby. I sent him running and he got tight with Petrini to the point of becoming his clerk."

Thorndyke finished his schooner of ale and called to Murphy for another. "He's probably done the same with Gutenberger. Olsen is shallow in the thinking department, Constable but is quick to take advantage of anyone. Sneaky little rat if you want my opinion. Watch your back."

"Doesn't sound like a murderer, Ben. Sounds like a confidence man, a fraudster." Kennedy stopped instantly and his mind went racing through what he said. *Is it even possible? Could that snake be the leader of this liquor scheme? Were these others cheating him? No, it just couldn't.*

"If you're thinking that the idea of what we call the liquor scheme was his, Constable, you might be on to something. It would be his way, but how he could involve the judge and a county commissioner is a long hard road to follow."

"Not with Gutenberger's help," Kennedy said. "I have enough evidence right now to arrest Petrini and Creighton on bribery charges if they weren't dead. I'm still sure that it was Peabody who arranged for Petrini's murder and he's dead. What makes this even more logical, Ben, I can't find Sven Olsen. Wherever he went, he didn't take his own mule and carriage, they're safe at his home."

Thorndyke said he had to get back to his store and Kennedy headed for the courthouse and his office. He was met by the two other county commissioners who informed him that they wanted him to suggest a name or two to replace Judge Petrini until an election could be held. "I'll give it some thought," he said. "Will someone be appointed to fill the remainder of Peabody's term?"

"We've discussed several names including Jacob Hoagland, but not settled on anyone," Commissioner Dudley said.

"I'll give that some thought as well," Kennedy said. Instead of going into his office, he took a long walk along the river to the Gutenberger warehouse and another meeting with Terrence Smith. *I simply don't understand where Sven Olsen fits in this picture.*

"Sorry to seem like a pest, Mr. Smith, but I need more of your time. What exactly is it that is kept in this warehouse?"

"Very little is kept, Constable. Produce and meats are brought in for shipment to other parts of the territory, the same as some manufactured items such as farm implements and wood products. On the other side of the coin, products are brought in for distribution in the Brookside area. Nothing sits in the warehouse for long."

"Give me a short tour, will you?"

"Give yourself a walk-through. I've got a shipment ready to send off as soon as that boat there gets docked."

This was far more than Kennedy hoped for, given carte blanch to search the large building for illegal liquor. There seemed to be no particular plan in the layout of aisles or in the distribution of product and the Constable just walked up one and down the next. "A barrel or two of Virginia rum should stand out, I'd have thought," he murmured.

When he got to the end of the building, he found a section covered in canvas and pulled a flap back to take a peek. "So! The barrels are emptied somewhere else, jugged and cased, and shipped here for distribution. And not a dime of tax is collected? How would one know?"

He knew that somewhere along the line there was a break in protocol. Import fees must be paid and tags attached verifying that, he had been told. "But that was for barrels. What about these bottles, jugs, and flasks? How would one know if the fees and taxes had been paid?" He picked up an earthen jug and inspected it, saw nothing that would tell anyone that the barrel it came in had passed through the tax man's gate.

He said good-bye to Smith and hurried back to town to see the county attorney. "Claude, I've found enough evidence to send many to prison, but I need some help. My God, do I need some help."

"You've worked up quite a sweat, my friend. Come in and have a brandy." Claude Atkins was actually out of bed, up on his feet, and walking for the first time in weeks. "Sit, Toby and tell me what you've found that has you in such a fit."

"I remember you telling me that when barrels of liquor are imported, and the taxes paid the barrels carry tags attesting to the taxes. Is that right?"

"Yes, just as I said," Atkins answered. "What have you found?"

"I've found cases of bottles of imported Virginia rum. Not barrels, Claude. Cases of bottles. How does one know if taxes have been paid?"

"Deception, deception, deception," Atkins chuckled with each repetition of the word. "A buyer of a barrel of liquor has the right then to bottle what he has, but he does have the right to sell that bottle. To be sold rum or other liquor must be sold as a barrel, keg, or bottle, but it must come with the proper tax stamps. Bottles are used in saloons, eh, and for home or office use. Is this the Gutenberger group?" Kennedy nodded and Atkins smiled.

"Once they get the barrels past the tax man they're bottling the stuff," Kennedy said. "Those I saw carried no stamps or other markings. Do those buying it know they are buying illicit merchandise?"

"You have a double-edged fraud going on here, Constable. Those selling and those buying are both breaking the law."

Kennedy sat, shaking his head. "This is far out of my jurisdiction, Claude. I can stop the operation here in Brookside, but it must begin where the ships are unloaded. That's where Gutenberger would be. I have to see to it that the territorial attorney is aware, Claude but I can't go."

"No you can't, but Ben Thorndyke can. He's already aware of what you've been doing because of the Creighton affair. Go see him, Toby."

CHAPTER 28

Kennedy bypassed Thorndyke in favor of a visit with County Assessor Conrad Shelley, the local tax man. The constable decided he would put in writing everything he knew about the importing and distribution of Virginia rum without benefit of taxes and fees being paid and send it to the territorial attorney.

I'll just concentrate on solving these murders and let them worry about the money end of things. My murderer is probably their tax evader. He had to chuckle at the thought. He stuck his head in the assessor's office at the courthouse only to be told that Shelley hadn't been in all day. Conrad Shelley lived on the very edge of Brookside, a good three miles from the courthouse and Kennedy saddled his horse for the short ride. Shelley was one of the first to make the long venture from the banks of the Missouri to the shores of the Pacific with the intent of staying. A pioneer in every respect.

The day was hot for so early in the spring and Kennedy wiped sweat from his brow. A fast trot through the drying streets cooled him off. Shelley's cabin was set back in a stand of tall fir trees. He was among the first of those settling in the valley and had never upgraded his self-hewn log cabin. Kennedy found Shelley's horse standing in a corral and the man's shay in a covered three-sided shed.

Pounding on the door, Kennedy called out. "It's Constable Kennedy, Shelley. We need to talk." There was no answer and the man walked around the small cabin, couldn't see in the curtained windows but found the rear door unlocked. He checked on the horse and found the water trough low and no hay scattered about.

Kennedy was well aware of Conrad Shelley's reputation of being a strong and willing worker. He built the cabin without help, brought every log from standing tree to firm wall, and was proud of being able to. This wasn't like the Shelley that Kennedy knew.

I shouldn't do this without someone being with me, he thought. Was he walking into a crime scene? Or invading someone's privacy? It would be best to have a second person as a witness. He gently pushed the door open. There was little light coming in and Kennedy found himself standing in what passed for a kitchen. The wood stove was cold to his touch.

"Doesn't seem anyone has been in here for a spell," he muttered. He walked into a second room, found an over-stuffed chair, clothes hanging on pegs, and a rope strung bed with a straw mattress. It was Conrad Shelley's bloated body on the bed that had his full attention.

"Another murder? The man who would have all the answers about import taxes and fees?" It took just minutes to find the cause of death. Just as lethal but not quite as brutal, the constable thought, looking at the bloody crushed bones in the middle of the man's head. A short handled four-pound hammer lay next to the body.

"Two with their heads bashed in and one knifed." He

opened the front door of the cabin and was able to see his boot prints in the dust and looked for others. They weren't hard to find. "Lumberjack boots again, but no blood spatters. He found a stick and notching it with his knife was able to get a fair measurement. Back inside, Kennedy looked for other signs of violence but found none.

Judge Petrini and Conrad Shelley were murdered by someone they knew well enough to invite into their homes. And it has to be the same person, which throws another of my ideas out the window. How could Slack-jaw have done this one? He's still locked up tight. Yet, he all but confessed to killing the judge.

Constable Kennedy spent more than an hour going through the cabin and finding little of significance. "Our Mr. Shelley lived a spartan life. If he was a part of this liquor fraud, you'd never know it from what he has here," he said right out loud. Shelley didn't even have a bottle or flask of Virginia rum in the cabin. He closed up the cabin and drove back to town to find Doctor Winslow and send him out.

Kennedy went to his office and got the safe open. He had all the papers from the little wall cabinet in the judge's office along with the papers from Creighton's place. He remembered Irene Creighton telling him that she had taught Ed Creighton the proper way to keep his accounts up to date.

Somebody was keeping the judge's books up to date, but they surely weren't accurate. Even I can see the discrepancies. He spent more than an hour working through various pages of numbers and taking notes. *It wasn't Judge Petrini skimming money off the top, it was whoever handled these books. The organization was coming up several thousand dollars short after every distribution of a new shipment.*

He was about to close up his work and was interrupted by Ned Walling. "I think I've found Sven Olsen, Constable. Are you familiar with Turkey Run Road? There's a cabin about seven miles up that road and Olsen is there with two other men."

"Let me get this back in the safe and we'll take a ride out there, Mr. Walling. Are you up to it?"

"I'm fine sir," the big timber man said.

TURKEY RUN ROAD CAME BY ITS MONIKER HONESTLY AS the wide canyon leading out of Brookside was home to several large flocks of turkey. Many families enjoyed the fruits of that canyon every year. The trail, it wasn't really a road. was not maintained and Kennedy decided it would be best if they rode their horses instead of taking a buggy or wagon.

He had Walling describe what he found as they made the seven-mile ride. "One of the men was dressed as a gentleman, Constable, that is, he was wearing a suit with starched collar and all. the other was a lumber jack for sure. Even had his climbing boots on."

Kennedy was hoping that the 'gentleman' would be Gutenberger and wondered just who the lumber jack might be. The thought that Slack-jaw Compton confessed to the Petrini murder and yet the killing of Conrad Shelley was a mirror image, clouded his mind.

The cabin was an old hunting lodge built ten or more years ago by a group of men who spent more time around the fire playing poker and drinking whiskey than they did hunting. It was used often by Petrini, Creighton, and their friends. Kennedy's immediate thought was that this was where most of the business was handled for the liquor fraud bunch.

As they turned off Turkey Run Road for the cabin Kennedy saw four horses in a makeshift corral and smoke coming from the cabin chimney. "I thought you said two men were with Olsen," Kennedy said.

"That's what I saw. Two men were standing near the corral there talking with Sven Olsen."

"The four horses in that corral tells me there might be four men inside right now. Stay back here with the horses. I'm going to try to get close enough to hear or see something." They dismounted and Kennedy made his way through thick stands of trees to the side of the cabin without a window. The ground was drying out but the leaf and twig layer on the ground was still wet enough to make the walk a quiet one. In the bare places it was muddy.

Kennedy sneaked around to the back side of the cabin, found the door closed but there was a window he could get close to. The sun was such that he didn't dare try to catch a quick glimpse and just got close enough to hopefully hear something from inside. The cabin walls were rough hewn logs, chinked with local mud, but the window was covered with rags as a curtain.

He put his ear as close as he could and heard voices that sounded like arguing, or at the least loud discussion. He couldn't understand enough to know what the argument was about. He carefully moved back to where Ned Walling stood with the horses.

"We'll just have to wait, Mr. Walling. From the way you described the men you saw, I take it you didn't recognize anyone."

"Only Sven Olsen. I don't know the other two. The one in climbing boots was a bruiser of a man, though. The other thin and slightly bent."

They sat down behind a fallen tree, were able to see

the cabin, and watched. It was times like this that Kennedy used his powerful mind to sort out what he was investigating. The thing with Slack-jaw and now another identical murder had the constable confused. He could not find the logic in the situation.

Compton said Peabody hired him and he in turn brought Upton in. Did he really say to kill Judge Petrini or was he only talking about burning my house down? Ah, ah, ah. When I get back my notes will tell me for certain. If Shelley had any personal papers they are gone now.

"Got some movement, Constable," Walling said. "Men coming out."

Kennedy crawled around the log to get a better view and saw four men walk toward the corral. Olsen shook hands with the man in the suit and stood back as the three brought their horses out and mounted. *Wish I could hear what they're saying.*

The three men rode up to Turkey Run Road and turned toward town. Sven Olsen walked back into the cabin. "Let's pay a little social call on the court clerk, shall we Mr. Walling?" It was a quick walk down to the cabin. "Keep an eye on the back door, Walling," and Kennedy pounded on the front door. "It's Constable Kennedy, Mr. Olsen. Open up, please." Olsen didn't answer nor did he come to the door. "I'll only ask one more time, sir. Open the door, Sven"

Kennedy was about to kick the door open when he heard a scuffle from the rear of the building and ran around to find Walling kneeling on Olsen's back, rubbing his face in the mud. "Thank you, Mr. Walling. That's enough now."

Kennedy jerked Olsen to his feet and pushed him back inside the cabin. "Have a seat, Sven, and we'll have a nice little chat." Kennedy took a look around the sparsely furnished one-room cabin and was amazed to find several cases of fine Virginia rum stacked in a corner. "Ah, I see we'll have something to wet our throats, Mr. Walling."

Ned Walling smiled as he pulled a bottle from a case. "This is expensive, Constable. Maybe we'd best not."

"let me see," Kennedy said taking the jug. It took less than the blink of an eye for Kennedy to know that import taxes had not been paid. "It seems you are in possession of some illegal liquor, Sven. That same liquor is why I'm having this little meeting with you." Kennedy sat down across the table from Olsen and opened the jug.

"I'm sure Mr. Olsen won't mind, will you?" he asked. Olsen was glaring, first at Walling and then at Kennedy but said nothing. He was dressed in a fine wool suit and on a peg was a new beaver hat trimmed with a silk hat band. "You're dressed for an occasion, Mr. Olsen. what would that be?"

Again, there was silence. Kennedy motioned for Walling to hand him some tin cups that were hanging on pegs near the stove and poured generously for them. "I've never tasted rum this smooth, Constable. A man could get used to drinking this."

"Let me see if I have some of this figured out, sir," Kennedy said, glaring into Olsen's eyes. "I believe that was John Gutenberger who just rode off with two of his henchmen, one of whom may have butchered your dear friend Conrad Shelley. Did Gutenberger come down here with orders for you to follow or to receive orders for him to follow? which is it, Olsen?"

"I don't know what you're talking about, Constable. there was no one here named Gutenberger. Who is that?"

196

"Come now, Olsen, let's not make this so difficult. I had a long talk with Terrence Smith at the warehouse this morning, saw the many cases of rum stacked along the north wall, the same as those cases over there." Kennedy pointed at the cases, but his eyes were demanding answers from the court clerk.

"Smith told me he got his orders from you. I know all about the liquor tax fraud scheme, sir, but what I'm looking to solve are the murders of three of our fine residents and I will break as many heads as I have to break to solve those killings." He bent over and shoved his face right up to Olsen's. "Do I make myself clear?"

Olsen pulled back as far as he could, trembled at the thought of Kennedy's fabled walking stick, but said nothing. He tried to close his eyes to the terror in his face and a got a good slap in the face for the effort. "You look at me when I'm talking to you, sir. You have lied to me too many times, Sven Olsen. You lied when you said the judge didn't drink. You lied about where the judge's personal records were."

Olsen sat motionless in the old bent wood chair, staring into space, barely breathing, shaking. He was startled when Ned Walling popped the cork on a bottle of rum, started to get up and Kennedy slammed him back into the chair. "Judge Petrini was one of the partners in this liquor tax scheme, Mr. Olsen, and so was Ed Creighton. Mr. Gutenberger was a third member of the organization, but there were more, weren't there, and you kept all the records."

Olsen knew he couldn't run, but also knew he had to get away. How? The door was closed tight, Walling was a huge man, Kennedy was bigger. "I don't know what you're talking about," he said again.

"Mr. Peabody knew the tax law well enough to allow

for the fraud. So did Mr. Shelley, but they're dead now. Their names are in your books, Olsen. Why was Gutenberger here and why did he bring two thugs with him? Was it because you were cheating him as well as all the other partners? Was he here to threaten you, Olsen?"

Olsen sat as still as an oak in a breeze, dared not look at Kennedy, dared not try to speak. He watched Walling pour two more drinks of rum and handed one to the constable. "Smells delicious, sir," he said.

Kennedy took his, wafted it under his slightly red nose, and took a drink. "Ah, Mr. Olsen, thank you for this delightful respite. You and your partners. Now, let's gets back to our discussion, eh? The books you kept, in your own hand, sir, indicate that you held back on your partners. Is that why you're killing them off, one at a time?"

Olsen sat quiet, wanted a full glass of what the two were enjoying, and stared at the door. "Well, maybe it would be better if we held this conversation back at the jail, eh Mr. Olsen? I'll have my fine walking stick in hand and you'll be tied to the iron bars of the jail cell, and you'll be more than willing to talk to me."

Kennedy walked about the cabin, noting where everything was. A table, several chairs, the cases of liquor, even a coat or two on iron hooks driven into the log walls. "When we get back, Mr. Walling, I'm appointing you to bring a small crew back out here to gather these cases of rum as evidence. Bring them to my office, and I've a good count," he chuckled. "Minus these two, of course."

Walling laughed and knew he would have a hard time getting it all back without having to fight off some of those helping him but agreed to the job. "Aye, Constable, I'll do my best."

"Let's get this party moving, then," Kennedy said. He jerked Olsen to his feet and shoved him toward the back door. "Go get our horses while I get this man tied onto his, Mr. Walling.

Olsen made a break for the corral as soon as Kennedy got the back door opened but didn't make the fourth step when a massive fist slammed him on the back of his head, and he found his face in the mud again. "You're a nasty little man, eh, Mr. Olsen? Well, sir, if you try that again, I'll have no recourse but to bring you into the courthouse tied feet and hands to a long pole. Your friends will find considerable mirth in that scene, I believe."

Kennedy jerked Olsen to his feet, turned him to face him, and punched him in the nose hard enough to get the blood flowing and the man floundering in the mud. "On your feet, Olsen, and into the saddle you go." Kennedy tied the man's hands behind his back and tied his feet to the stirrups and led the horse from the corral.

On a late spring afternoon, the streets of Brookside were filled with people out enjoying the warmth. Kennedy made a fine showing of it, bringing Sven Olsen right up to the courthouse steps and untying him before jerking him off the horse. "See to the horses, will you, Mr. Walling? I'll see to our prisoner."

CHAPTER 29

"I swear, Mr. Thorndyke, Constable Kennedy just brought Sven Olsen to jail, trussed up like a feral hog." Peter Johansen was out of breath having run the entire way to Thorndyke's emporium.

"Thank you, Peter," Ben Thorndyke said. "Here's two bits for your trouble." Ben put on a light coat and walked down to the courthouse, enjoying the bright sun. "Looks like Toby may have found some of his answers." Thorndyke loved to walk fast and have great conversations with himself. "My God, three murders in this little village. Creighton's death isn't related to any of this, but he was. I wonder if Kennedy has looked into the possible land fraud that Creighton and Gutenberger were engaged in?"

He sent a message to Governor Henry Raymond about that and found it odd that he hadn't heard back. Kennedy's office was empty when Ben walked in but heard noises in the back where the holding cells were. "You in there, Constable?"

"Yes, Ben, come in. There's more bad news I'm afraid." Ben found Slack-jaw Compton in one cell and

Sven Olsen in another. They were separated by an empty cell. "Our county assessor, Conrad Shelley was murdered, Ben. Seems it's a dangerous business, this tax fraud business. I believe you know Court Clerk Sven Olsen."

Ben chuckled as they left the cell area. "You've made considerable progress, it seems."

"Sit, Ben and we'll talk. I've a good handle on the liquor scheme but I've run myself into a rock wall as far as the murders go. Judge Petrini was killed by blows to the head with a heavy hammer as was Conrad Shelley. It appears that both men knew the killer to the point of inviting them into their homes. Clyde Peacock on the other hand was slashed and stabbed with a knife in his office after what appeared to be an altercation."

"Are you saying we may have two killers running around our town?" Ben Thorndyke asked. He seemed astounded by the idea and stood up, took a step or two and sat backdown. "Tell me more."

"It is possible we may have two killers, yes, but it's also possible that the killings aren't related. That's the mess I'm in right now. Slack-jaw Compton has all but confessed to killing judge Petrini. If that's so, who killed Shelley in almost the exact way Petrini was killed?" Kennedy threw some wood in the stove and poured coffee for the two. "Peacock and Shelley were both murdered while Slack-jaw was behind bars."

"Why do you have Sven Olsen in jail?" Ben asked.

"Partly because he is tied tight to the liquor fraud scheme, but I believe he either killed Commissioner Peabody or arranged for it."

"Oh, my." Thorndyke took a long drink of coffee. "He's underhanded, lies with ease, and as untrustworthy as any man I've ever met, but a killer? A knife wielding killer?"

"He's been stealing thousands of dollars from the liquor fraud gang, Ben, and I think they caught on. that's what precipitated the murders. I'm not sure he killed Petrini and Shelley. I think he hired someone for that but I'm pretty sure he killed Peacock. Proving all this will be my next big job."

"I'm going to leave you to it, Toby. I've got to get back to the store." Thorndyke left and Kennedy once again got all the paperwork from his safe and spread out on his desk. He also got the Slack-jaw file out and read his notes. He walked back into the cell area and brought Slack-jaw into the office.

"Up for another little talk, Mr. Compton?" He had his knotted walking stick in hand. We need a bit of clarification. I'd rather not hang a man if he is innocent. Tell me again how it was you were working for Commissioner Peacock and what exactly you did."

"Why do you got that fool Sven Olsen in jail? He's da one who told Peacock what to do and Peacock paid me to do it."

"To do what, exactly, Slack-jaw?" Kennedy asked. *Maybe I'm coming close. So again someone tells me that Olsen gives the orders and despite having all the papers from that little cabinet, Olsen's name doesn't appear. Why does he give the orders?*

Before he could answer a man ran into the office. "Come quick, Constable. Mrs. Creighton is in trouble."

"Oh, my God," Kennedy said. He hustled Slack-jaw back in his cell and ran for the door. "At her home?" The man nodded and pointed, and Kennedy ran the two blocks to the Creighton home. The front door had been splintered and was standing open. Several neighbors and passers-by were trying to get a glimpse of what was inside the doorway.

"Move aside, now. Move aside." Kennedy bawled it out manhandling people out of the way. He carefully stepped around pieces of the door and found Irene Creighton on the floor of the front room, sobbing. Little Carrie was alongside, bleeding from a bash on the head.

Kennedy was on. his knees, looked at the girl, saw she was breathing and called out the door for someone to bring the doctor. "Mrs. Creighton, It's Tobias Kennedy at your side. The doctor is coming. What happened here?"

"Two men, Constable. They broke down the door and hit Carrie with something and tore my house apart. Look," she said. Tables were overturned, bookcases were ravaged, broken glass and pottery covered the floor.

"Was anything said?" Kennedy was using his kerchief to stem the blood flow from Carrie's head wound. The little girl was gaining consciousness and started whimpering. Irene took her up in her arms and held her tight. Never mind the blood.

"One of the men hit me hard, Constable and demanded to know where their money was. They were going to kill me," she cried it out. "They said Mr. Creighton owed them and they would take it out on me and my baby."

Kennedy wondered if he knew who the two men were. Were they with who he thought was Gutenberger at the Turkey Run cabin? They looked like thugs and he looked at the splintered door. Either could do that kind of damage. "Can you give me a quick description of the two men, Mrs. Creighton? I may know who they are."

"One, the big man who hit me and Carrie, was dressed as a lumber jack but the other was a well dressed man, thin and walked with a limp."

Doctor Winslow arrived and Kennedy again had to move the small crowd back from the open front door. "Now stay back or I'll have you all in my little jail for the night." He walked back into the front room. "How is the girl, Doctor? She was bleeding heavy when I got here."

"She got hit hard, but she'll be fine. Head wounds do bleed heavy." Winslow turned to Irene. "Were you hit, too, Mrs. Creighton? I mean besides the eye." The area around her left eye was starting to turn purple from the blow she took.

"He hit me in the ribs with a cudgel, Doctor. It hurts to breathe."

"Is there someone who can stay with you? I'll want to have a good look, but I'd bet you have a broken rib or two." The doctor moved his fingers along the side of Irene's chest, which caused her to cry out.

"I'm here, and I'll see to it that she's taken care of." Beverly Thorndyke walked into the room along with her son Gerald. Gerald got right down on his knees and took Carrie's hand. "Gerald, let's get the two of them into bed. Doctor, leave what you think they'll need. We'll take over now."

Winslow chuckled which told Kennedy that things would be just fine at the Creighton home.

Kennedy had to chuckle as Beverly moved Doctor Winslow aside and eased Irene to her feet. "Bring Carrie, Gerald. Constable, you'll have to wait a spell before you can ask any more questions. These girls need my attention."

"Yes Ma'am," Kennedy said. Doctor Winslow said something under his breath that couldn't be deciphered. "I'll be back a little later," Kennedy said. He walked back to his office, a million thoughts working in his head.

A thin little man who walked with a limp and a big man

dressed for forest work. It had to be Gutenberger and one of the thugs he had with him at the cabin. All these men can think of is money. They had to be looking for that little wooden box that Mrs. Creighton found. My God they could have killed that child.

Anger was at the boiling point by the time Kennedy reached the courthouse and sat at his desk. There was a loud knock at the door and a large man walked in. "You!" Kennedy exploded from his chair and grabbed that knotted walking stick. "Just what have you done? If that little girl dies, I'll hang you myself."

He was about to whack the large man who cried out, "No, Constable, it wasn't me. Let me explain, sir."

"You've got less than one minute to make yourself known." Kennedy held that oak rod at the ready, motioned the man inside and told him to sit down. "If that little girl dies because of you there might not be much left to hang."

"How is it you seem to recognize me. I've just arrived in Brookside," the man said.

"Lying to me will get you a severe thrashing sir. I saw you with Sven Olsen at the Turkey Run Road camp. Don't deny it." He got right down in the man's face. "I saw you."

The large man smiled and started to reach inside his jacket. "No, no, Sir," Kennedy said, that heavy stick ready to strike. Was he going for a knife?

"I've something you need to see, Constable. Please."

"Nice and easy, fella, or it's off to sleep with you."

The large man slowly opened his coat and with one hand puled a folded leather wallet from an inside pocket. "My name is Oscar Levant," he said, handing the piece to Kennedy. "I'm an investigator for the Oregon Territorial Attorney General. I am here to find enough evidence of tax fraud to arrest several people, including John Guten-berger, the man you saw me with earlier."

Kennedy looked at the official shield and identifica-tion of the man, smiled slightly, and sat down behind his desk. "Welcome to Brookside," he said. He drummed his fingers on the desktop trying to hide his pleasure at having this man from Oregon City in his office. *Just what I've been hoping for. Now I can concentrate on these murders and let this man worry about unpaid taxes. Four dead, three of them murdered, and all related in some way to those unpaid taxes.*

"I have two men back there behind bars you'll need to talk to, but many of those involved in the tax fraud are dead. Are you also looking into a land fraud scheme I've been told about?" Kennedy was smiling, not growling at the man.

"Yes I am. Gutenberger has no idea who I am and I'd like to keep it that way for at least another day or two. Tell me about these dead people. Up in Oregon City we don't get the news from Brookside very often."

"Probably many of those you came to investigate. Judge Anthony Petrini, one of the lead men, County Commissioner Clyde Peabody, and County Assessor Conrad Shelley. Petrini and Shelley were killed by vicious hammer blows to the head and Peabody was knifed."

Levant sat still for a moment, a smile slowly taking shape. "That almost wipes out the gang, Constable," Levant chuckled. "Got a line on the killer?"

"I thought I did," Kennedy said. He couldn't hide his rueful smile and explained his dilemma. "A man named Slack-jaw Compton said he was hired by Peacock to kill the judge, but he was in jail when Shelley was killed, and the two men died in almost exactly the same way. It's confusing." He got up and threw some wood in the stove and poured them some coffee. "The liquor tax fraud case is rather simple but what about the land fraud scheme I keep hearing about? This is a big territory and people come to better themselves. Land is here and is available for those willing to work for it."

"That's the key for the criminals, Constable. That's the opening that Gutenberger and his partner, Ed Creighton needed to work their fraud. The land is there and I can show you paperwork that says a parcel was homesteaded, legally, but in reality was sold by Gutenberger with help from Creighton."

"It's starting to make a little sense," Kennedy muttered. "Gutenberger and the other thug attacked Mrs. Creighton looking for money they believed Creighton held out from them. I think the man who actually held back is behind bars right now." Kennedy jerked his thumb toward the back room. "There's another man You need to meet and listen to."

Kennedy slipped into the cell area and brought Slack-jaw Compton into the office, pushed him into a chair, and grabbed up his walking stick. "Inspector, meet Slack-jaw Compton." Kennedy stuffed another log in the stove and stood in front of Compton. "Now, where were we when we got interrupted, sir? Ah, yes, you and Peacock."

He paced around for a few seconds before continuing. "You need to tell me again exactly what it was that Peacock paid you to do. Don't lie, Slack-jaw. I hate liars. Did he hire you to kill Judge Petrini?"

"No, Constable. I told you, he wanted me to burn your house down and I brought Ted with me. No, I ain't killed nobody."

Kennedy thumped the hard oak staff into his open

hand a time or two, glaring at Compton and finally moved him back into his cell. "That's my dilemma, Inspector. I was sure Slack-jaw killed the judge but when the county assessor turned up dead, killed in exactly the same way, I knew I was wrong."

He spent a little more time detailing what he knew about Sven Olsen and the many questions he had about just how Olsen fit into the picture. Levant listened and had a thought of his own. "Gurenberger was here to meet with Olsen to get answers about large sums of money that seemed to be missing. He wanted to know more about the man, Smith, the manager of the warehouse here in Brookside. He doesn't trust Smith. What's your call on that, Constable?"

"Are you still planning to stay undercover, Inspector? Because, if not, I know a little place that serves fine lamb and has a back bar filled with the nectar of the gods. We have a lot to talk about."

Levant's roar of laughter could be heard on the second floor of the courthouse and the two men were seen almost scurrying down the street to Murphy's Inn and Tavern. "If you are a regular customer, Constable, I doubt very many criminals infest the place. My being undercover won't be given away."

CHAPTER 30

The two big men spent several hours eating, drinking, and discussing the cases they were working on. Murders, tax fraud, land fraud, and an unprovoked attack on a lady and her child in her own home. "I'll blister that man's head, Levant. He'll never raise a hand to a woman again."

"He's been working with Gutenberger for some time and is wanted in several districts. Tell me what happened at the Creighton home. I hope you understand I had nothing to do with that."

"I'm sure," Kennedy said. "They actually broke down the door and attacked the little girl first, hitting her in the head with something hard and heavy, then attacked Mrs. Creighton. They were demanding money that they said Creighton owed them. I believe I have that money in my safe at the office."

"Creighton had sold a couple of large pieces of land but had not sent all the money on to Gutenberger. Crooks robbing crooks," Levant said.

"That's what precipitated the murders here in Brookside," Kennedy said. "Sven Olsen is a name you'll come to know very well. He's slimy, Inspector. The original idea to import Virginia rum and other expensive liquor without paying the import duty was probably Judge Petrini's. He along with a tax auditor in Oregon City and commissioner Peacock were organizing the deal and Gutenberger was brought in because of his knowledge of distribution. I think you know all that."

"That is my understanding, But, where does Olsen come in?" Levant asked.

"Petrini is to blame. He assumed that crooks don't cheat each other. That's a good one, eh? Sven Olsen was his court clerk and he got Olsen to do most of the leg work, keep the books, see to it that things moved according to plan. Olsen, the sneaky little varmint, took over, created his own plan, and saw to it that the others got just enough money to keep them satisfied. The rest went in his pocket." Kennedy could see the plan almost as if it were in written form in front of him.

"Is that when he cheated Terrence Smith? Is that when things went awry." Levant asked

"Smith? At the warehouse?" Kennedy sat bolt upright at the comment. "I thought he just worked for Gutenberger. This is new, Levant. Keep going, please."

Kennedy was more surprised than he had been in a long time. The man who ate too many beans was also in this plot? "Smith runs Gutenberger's warehouse but I hadn't heard any of this."

"Smith got a cut for keeping his mouth shut. The same for Shelley. Smith complained to Peacock that he was being shorted and Peacock traced it back to Petrini. Of course, it wasn't Petrini. As you say, it was Olsen but no one knew that. It was Smith, not Slack-jaw Compton who killed the judge and Shelley. You were right that

Compton was hired to burn you out." Levant was putting things in order as well.

"Who gave the order to kill the judge and Shelley? I believe it was Olsen," Kennedy said. "He wormed his way into running the operation without anyone knowing it."

"Exactly," Levant said. "As you said earlier, Constable, Olsen gave orders in Gutenberger's name. In Petrini's name. Even in Peacock's name, but no one knew that. When questions of missing money arose, Olsen saw to it that Petrini and Creighton were to blame and ordered Smith to kill Petrini. In Gutenberger's name, of course. Creighton was already dead."

"I have Olsen behind bars but if Gutenberger and his thug are on the loose here in Brookside, we have to protect him. We need to protect Mrs. Creighton, too," Kennedy said. "That man will be in a rage if he puts it all together."

"Let's get Smith behind bars first, Mr. Kennedy. Smith is far more dangerous than Gutenberger. If Smith figures out that he's been set up by Olsen, then both Olsen and Gutenberger will die."

Kennedy motioned to Ned Walling at the end of the bar. "Another little job, Ned, if you're up it. Inspector Levant and I are going to roust Terrence Smith and we could use your help."

Walling's eyes got big and he pointed at the inspector. "That's one of the men who was with Sven Olsen," Walling said. He stood back half a step. "You said inspector?"

"I'll explain as we go," Kennedy chuckled. "Just be prepared for some physical action."

. . .

"OH, BEN, IT WAS TERRIBLE," BEVERLY THORNDYKE CRIED, throwing her arms around her robust husband. "That poor little girl's head was bloody. Irene has a black eye and broken ribs. Those were horrible men."

"You were wonderful, Bev. I think we should see to it that Irene and little Carrie are safe. Somebody needs to be with them. A large aggressive somebody," Ben said. "I can't imagine how such a simple thing as tax evasion has grown to include murders and attacks on women and children."

"Who could we get who could face men like that?" Beverly asked.

"I don't know. I'm going to find the constable. This would be his call anyway," Thorndyke said. "I'm sure to find him at Murphy's this time of the evening."

Thorndyke enjoyed walking, even more so now that it really was spring. He had been aware of the over-all situation almost from the beginning because of Judge Petrini's stand with little Jeremy Creighton, had visited his old employee, the territorial governor on behalf of Irene Creighton, and wondered just what was really going on in his little community. There was no moon and the air was clean with a slight chill to it as the leading businessman of Brookside continued putting things together.

I've heard rumors of illegal land purchases, the governor told me about that, but what is behind these murders? Selling untaxed liquor would bring in considerable money, I'm sure. I hope Constable Kennedy is up to all this.

"Ah, Mr. Thorndyke," Murphy said. "No, you just missed him. He left in a bit of a hurry and didn't say where he was going. That was a fine thing your wife did, taking care of Mrs. Creighton. Have a brandy?"

"Well, since I'm here, yes, I believe I will. You've got

your ear to the community, Murph. What do you make of all this violence? Brookside has always been most peaceful."

"Aye, it has that," Murphy said. "Constable Kennedy said that it's a war inside a group of criminals, that it shouldn't affect me and the missus. I'm not so sure, though. Not since Mrs. Creighton was attacked."

"Kennedy's sure Ed Creighton was a part of that criminal activity," Ben said. "Definitely a tangled web of illegal activity. My wife and I are worried about Mrs. Creighton. She's alone and those men are running loose."

"Follow me," Murphy said and led them into the dining area where several loggers were having an early supper at the family table. "Gentlemen," Murphy said. "The widow Creighton was attacked earlier today, as you well know. Her daughter suffered a blow to the head as well. That dear lady and her daughter are alone in a house with a smashed in door and the men who attacked her are on the loose. She needs help."

As a man, the four loggers stood up and walked out the door, whacking Murphy on the shoulders. "I believe Mrs. Creighton will be as safe as a babe in your arms, Ben Thorndyke," Murphy chuckled. "Let's have another brandy, eh?"

"Indeed, sir. See to it those men get drinks and a meal on me, will you?"

"LOOKS LIKE A MEETING GOING ON," KENNEDY SAID AS THE three moved through the shadows toward the Gutenberger warehouse. The shutters at the warehouse office were open on a cool spring evening and the three got as close as they dared. It was a dark night, no moon to speak of and enough of a breeze to be heard gently whistling through the dense trees.

"That dolt of a constable is going to destroy what we've worked so hard for," John Gutenberger said. He was standing in front of the desk, glowering at Terrence Smith. "If Petrini wasn't stealing from us, who was? We got nothing from that Creighton woman. Borokopf was too eager to bash heads, so I never got to ask a single question."

"He's an animal, John. Judge Petrini swore on a bible that he was not stealing from us before I killed him." Terrence Smith no longer spoke with a slight German accent.

"Smith is one of the leaders, Levant. Did you pick up on that?" Kennedy was whispering. "He's been directing all this but didn't understand how low-down and rotten Sven Olsen was."

"Let's listen for another minute or two then arrest them," Levant said. "We might learn even more."

"I have just sold several tracts of land in the eastern parts of the territory and that money will be coming in soon." Gutenberger was still angry. "I'm having it sent directly to the warehouse. I think we need to ease up on our liquor distributing and concentrate on land sales, Terrence."

"I agree, John, but we also have to find that missing money. Thousands of dollars can't just disappear. Where was the leak?"

"It all falls back on Petrini," Gutenberger said. "He brought that little weasel in, Olsen, and that's when we started coming up short. We thought it was Petrini. The county assessor was also involved with Olsen. That man needs to die and soon."

"I agree, Gutenberger, but not before we find our

money. I'll start eliminating the need for this warehouse and the others, shut down the distributing end of our company, and we'll concentrate on land sales. The Snake River area is primed for large land sales if we don't mention words like Shoshone or Indian," Terrence Smith laughed.

"Now," Kennedy said, and the three rushed through the wide doors and into the office. "Don't move, gentlemen," he said.

Smith lunged across the desk and was met by Ned Walling's heavy body. Walling wrapped his arms around Smith's head and wrenched hard, trying to throw Smith to the ground. Instead, he snapped the big man's neck. Gutenberger didn't move, frozen in fright, terrorized by the sight of his dead partner falling to the floor.

Inspector Levant took the walking stick from Gutenberger and placed a large hand on the man's shoulder, grasping hard enough to get a cry from the little man. "You're under arrest, John Gutenberger. I'll take ten minutes or so to explain the charges when we get you comfortable and warm behind iron bars."

"Well done, gentlemen," Kennedy said. "We'll get this fine specimen locked up, have Shorty Salinsky pick up the body, and then, Inspector, you and I will spend the next several days going through every square inch of every building this mob has been attached to. So many people involved but only two left alive to face the wrath of Lady Justice." There was considerable irony in Kennedy's chuckle.

"We will need to keep Gutenberger and Olsen well separated, Constable." Levant said.

"Aye, we will. I wonder now. I was sure that Gutenberger was calling the shots, then changed my mind to believe that it was Olsen. Then I heard Smith calling the shots. I'm going out on a long limb, Inspector and say that Petrini thought he was the boss, but our little weasel Olsen took over and remained the one without these others knowing it. Smith thought he was, but Gutenberger unknowingly allowed Olsen to be."

"It makes sense but we'll know when we find the missing money," Levant said.

Kennedy smiled. "Accordong to a little black book that Ed Creighton used as a ledger, there's an account in a bank in Oregon City that holds thousands of dollars, so that will be part of it. Olsen has hidden the rest somewhere."

CHAPTER 31

Brookside was abuzz the next morning when word spread of the arrests and another death. Rumors flowed like the Willamette River at spring flood. Was the widow Creighton involved? My goodness, Sven Olsen is a criminal? Who the hell is John Gutenberger?

"We have been so intent on capturing Gutenberger that we have neglected the thug who attacked Mrs. Creighton," Kennedy said, pouring coffee for he and Levant. Walling sat quiet, nursing a cold cup, shaking his head when more was offered.

"You did what had to be done, Ned," Kennedy said.

"Yes, Constable, I understand all that, but it remains, I have now killed two men. It's what brutes do. What thugs do. I'm neither."

"You're an upstanding citizen, Mr. Walling," Oscar Levant said. "Oregon Territory could use more like you. The territory should be proud of men like you. I am."

Walling tried to smile his thanks and took his second cup of coffee. "It's just hard to accept. Killing another human being is against everything I've been taught. All my life. I don't want this to become acceptable."

217

"You've performed a wonderful service for Brookside and Oregon, Walling," Kennedy said. "Go back to being a logger, and the next time someone asks for your help, say no."

Walling laughed. "I would never be able to do that, Constable. That's the problem, really, isn't it? You needed help and I helped. Ask again, and the answer will be the same."

"Proving what I said about being a fine citizen," Levant said. "Now, Constable, let's concentrate on what you said earlier. The man who attacked Mrs. Creighton and her daughter is named Borokopf, an Oregon City troublemaker and wanted man. He's sure to know that Gutenberger is in jail and probably hasn't been paid. He'll be needing money."

"That man is dangerous," Walling said. "To attack a woman and child is despicable."

"He needs to be caught and we need to find where Mr. Olsen has a considerable stash of money hidden. Probably papers saying where it came from as well." Kennedy shoved more wood in the stove and paced around the small office. "Maybe we should just ask," he said.

"We know what Borokopf looks like, we've all seen him," Inspector Levant said. "Why not walk around town and chat it up with the people? He'll need food and money. We can meet back here in an hour."

The three left the office and split up, walking the slowly drying streets, talking with anyone out and about. Borokopf had been seen scrounging behind the bakery, had asked for directions to the Gutenberger warehouse, and had threatened one man who chased him off with his flintlock musket.

"We'll do better on horseback, I think," Kennedy said.

"Let's saddle up and ride together. We'll start at the warehouse."

As they mounted their horses a man ran up. "There's trouble at the widow Creighton's Constable," he cried out. The three put heels to horse hide and raced the short two blocks arriving in time to see two loggers holding a large man while another beat him about the face and head.

"Let's let the fool live, gentlemen," Kennedy cried out, stepping off his sliding horse. "That's the man we're hunting for."

Levant tied Borokopf's hands behind his back, put a rope around his neck and stepped back in the saddle. "If you run off, Joe, you'll get three steps before I jerk the rope and break your neck. Let's walk back to the courthouse, shall we?"

Irene Creighton stepped out of the house and pointed at Borokopf. "That's the man, Constable. He's the one who hit Carrie and me." One of the loggers put an arm around the lady and took her back into the house.

"We've got a fire going, Constable, and we'll have breakfast with the ladies before we repair the damage to her doorway." One of the loggers said as Kennedy followed Levant and Borokopf back to the courthouse.

"Take good care of that lady, men. She's been through much these last few months. Get the doctor if you think it's needed," Kennedy said.

IT WAS SEVERAL HOURS LATER THAT CONSTABLE KENNEDY found himself alone in his office, a stack of papers from his safe spread across his desk. *I should be a happy man*, he thought, eyeing the papers and hearing noise from the cell area. *Mr. Gutenberger thought that Terrence Smith had brought Sven Olsen into the gang while Smith was sure that Gutenberger had. Olsen had both of them taking his orders thinking they were coming from the other. He was amassing large amounts of money that had to be hidden somewhere.*

Kennedy spent most of the late afternoon going over every scrap of paper on his desk and coming up with no answers. At last, he went back to the safe and pulled the little box from Ed Creighton's place. The money of course held no answers, but there were notes and memos in the box as well.

Most of what he read were notes on how much each land sale would bring the partners and how much Ed Creighton planned to hold out for himself. Kennedy held one small sheet of paper and read it over two or three times. *Mr. Creighton apparently saw where, who he thought was Petrini, was holding out on the liquor fraud payments to the partners. Creighton thought the money was being hidden at the hunting lodge on Turkey Run Road.*

Kennedy walked back into the cell area. "Mr. Gutenberger, I'd like to have a quiet word or two with you," he said. Kennedy unlocked the cell and ushered the man into the front office. "This shouldn't take long, sir, and you can get back to the comfort of your cell." He didn't attempt to hold back the nasty snicker.

He told the man to sit, put some wood in the fire and poured himself a cup of coffee. He sat behind his desk, found his flask in the left hand bottom drawer, and poured some brandy in his cup. He picked up his knotted oak walking stick and thumped it hard on top of his desk, which caused Gutenberger to stiffen, almost cringe.

"Nasty little piece of fine hardwood, isn't it?" Kennedy

said. "Raises terrible welts and bruises. Has been known to induce bleeding on occasion. I'm a man who believes in truth, Mr. Gutenberger. To lie is a sin I won't tolerate. Do we understand each other?" For emphasis he thumped the desk again and Gutenberger jumped back in fear.

"That's a rather worn down shack that Judge Petrini called his hunting lodge, eh? You and the judge meet there often?"

Gutenberger sat silent, sweat forming on his brow and fear flashing from his eyes. The rap on his knees from that walking stick came faster than the eye could follow and Gutenberger's scream would have been heard on the second floor of the courthouse if it wasn't so late in the evening.

"Again, sir. You and the judge meet there often?"

"From time-to-time." Gutenberger was almost sobbing in pain. The knob on the end of that walking stick ripped a gash in his knee and the pain seared. Gutenberger had his eyes on the flask of brandy, could almost taste it each time the constable took a sip. Kennedy smiled with each sip, blew gently across the cup, letting the aroma fill the office.

"Why were you meeting with Sven Olsen, the judge's clerk?" Gutenberger didn't answer, just stared at the wall behind Kennedy. "Olsen call the meeting?" Again, no answer. "Maybe it was Terrence Smith who called the meeting."

This time the walking stick smashed into the man's shin bone and Gutenberger screamed. "Smith sent me information through Olsen, yes."

Kennedy smiled knowing that from this moment forward he owned John Gutenberger. He would get whatever answers he wanted. "Why not just straight to you from him? Seems odd that Olsen would even be in the loop."

"Yes, it was, but that's what Smith wanted."

"And you sent information back to Smith through Olsen?"

"At Smith's request, yes," Gutenberger said. Gutenberger couldn't answer faster.

"I'm still interested in that shabby cabin where you met. Smith wasn't there. Only Olsen. Why wasn't Mr. Smith there?"

"I don't know." Gutenberger seemed confused. "We were supposed to talk about one of our businesses, but Olsen said Smith wasn't feeling well. Olsen gave me a letter from Smith telling us that Ed Creighton had been holding out and his widow had the money." Gutenberger realized what he'd just said and clammed up immediately. He wouldn't look at Kennedy.

The cudgel slammed into Gutenberger's knee again and the man was reduced to a sobbing, bleeding, loser. Kennedy had a wicked smile on his face as he added some brandy to his empty coffee cup. "Thank you, Mr. Gutenberger. Oh, by the way, is there a root cellar at that hunting lodge?"

"It's where Smith often held barrels of rum before bottling, I believe." Gutenberger spat it out between sobs. "In the side of the hill behind the corrals, it's a cool and dry cave hidden by some heavy brambles."

Kennedy hustled Gutenberger back to his cell. He was limping and crying out in pain with every step. "You've been very helpful, sir. According to Inspector Levant, a judge is being sent our way from Oregon City, so you will all be tried right here in Brookside. I'll have your supper sent over shortly, gentlemen."

CHAPTER 32

Inspector Levant muscled his way through the brambles with Constable Kennedy and Ned Walling right behind. It was raining, the brambles had thorns half an inch long and the footing was slick. "Your idea to put me in front, Constable?" Levant asked.

"You seemed to want to be there," Kennedy laughed. "I suggested we use the ax but you were in too big a hurry."

"Yeah, yeah. I can see the opening. How in the name of hades did they get barrels of rum through these bushes?"

"Gutenberger said that Smith said that. I expect that Olsen told Gutenberger that Smith said that. I think we'll find a hoard of money tucked in the back of that cave, not barrels of rum. Remember, there were cases of rum in the cabin, not barrels. Olsen had Smith and Gutenberger dancing on strings my friend. Whatever he wanted done or said, all he had to do was say one of those two wanted it."

Levant mixed a couple of nasty words with a chuckle and got the last of the brambles cut away and the three walked into a dry cave. Kennedy lit a torch he had brought and they found candles sticking from the walls and lit them. "Oh, my," is all Kennedy could say.

There were four stout wooden boxes, their lids off to the side, and gold coins showing, lined up against a rock wall. Kennedy hefted one box. "Must weigh fifty pounds, Inspector and there are four of them. Two hundred pounds of gold coins." Kennedy grabbed up his torch from the wall and walked toward the back of the cave.

"Mr. Olsen was about to pull the plug. He has a trunk back here filled with new and rather fine clothing. If we hadn't taken him into custody the other day, he would be long gone. That meeting was to put everyone's attention on Gutenberger. He knew Gutenberger would in turn bring Smith into the picture. He'd be in California heading for the port of San Francisco by now."

Kennedy dragged the trunk out near the boxes of gold. "Mr. Walling, ride back to town and harness my team and bring the wagon out here. Inspector Levant and I will get all of this out and ready for you by the time you get back."

The inspector gave a long, grave look at Kennedy but had to break it off with a sigh. "Well of course we will," he muttered. After Walling left Kennedy motioned for Levant to follow him.

"We've cut a fine path through the brambles, Inspector and I think there's a wheelbarrow in the shed there. We'll have those crates moved and have time for a smoke, too, sir." Levant chuckled at the comment.

"You had that all planned, eh?"

JACOB HOAGLAND AND HIS SON LUCAS WERE PLANTING the recently acquired hundred acres when County

Commissioner Amos Dudley drove his cart out. "Good morning, Commissioner," Jacob said. "What brings you out from behind your bank's doors? Offering me another loan are you?"

"No, Jacob, No I'm not," Dudley laughed. "I'm here on county business this morning. I need an hour or more of your time, I'm afraid. It is important."

"This isn't the right time for me to quit what I'm doing," Jacob said. He saw Dudley's serious face, looked over at Lucas and knew the boy was too young and inexperienced to do the seeding alone, and shook his head.

"Listen to me, Hoagland. The county needs you and I'm not leaving until we've had a chance to have a long conversation. Please, sir." Jacob looked at Luke, back at the banker, saw acres of open ground that needed seeding and nodded.

"If it's that important, all right. I'll ride up to the house with you."

"I'll unhitch the mules and bring them home," Lucas said.

It was a fast ride with Dudley driving his pacer at a quick trot the whole way. "Our little county is in a fix, Mr. Hoagland, and Commissioner Conroy and I have spent some time on this. I believe you know that Commissioner Peacock was killed recently in that ugly scheme perpetrated by Judge Petrini."

Dudley drove the buggy to the kitchen porch and the two continued their conversation as they walked into the house. "Yes. Martha and I are friends with Irene Creighton. That dear lady has had a rough row to hoe, I'm afraid. Let's sit at the kitchen table, Commissioner. It's always a more friendly place than the stuffy front room. Ah, Martha has a full pot of coffee waiting for us. Thank you, sweetheart."

"I'll leave you two alone now," Martha said.

"Please, Mrs. Hoagland, I think it might be best if you stayed. What I'm here to discuss will involve the two or you," Dudley said. She looked to Jacob before giving her nod and brought the coffee pot over to the kitchen table along with a basket of fresh bread.

"Where's Lucas?" She asked.

"He's bringing the mules in. Be here shortly," Jacob said. "Now, Commissioner, what's this all about?"

"Brookside County government is operated by three county commissioners but at the moment we have but two, which as you can imagine won't work," Dudley said. "Peter Conroy and I have discussed this with Constable Kennedy, Ben Thorndyke, and others in the community, and everyone is in agreement that you would be a fine replacement for Peacock. Your appointment would fill the seat until the end of his regular term in two years."

"Oh, my," Jacob said. He was stunned by the offer, looked at Martha who sat with her mouth half open, as if not being able to speak. "Why would you offer such a position to me? I've never given a thought to politics. Most often, I've stayed far away from those who love to argue constantly over subjects they know little about."

Dudley laughed and nodded at the comment. "You're a fair man, Jacob, a fine farmer and rancher, a good family man. In fact, an upstanding citizen of Oregon Territory. Many in the community like the idea of the commission representing various facets of what the community itself is made of. Business, timber, and ranching. Those three areas are Brookside. Whether or not you would want to run for election in two years would be your decision, but right now, we need someone of your ilk on the board."

"I think it's a wonderful idea," Martha said. Her

cheeks reddened some realizing that she had broken into their conversation. She brought a bowl of jam to the table and sat down.

"I'm not sure I do," Jacob said. "My God, Martha. How could I devote any time at all to being a county commissioner when I don't have enough time to take care of our ranch?" He turned his attention to the banker. "How could you ask such a thing of a man?"

"Mr. Conroy owns a lumber mill, Jacob. One of the busiest in the area, and often attends our meetings still dressed in work clothes and covered in saw-dust. I'm a banker and more than once I've left work on the bank's desk in order to attend to county business. No, Hoagland, it isn't always pleasant, but we only meet twice a month for just a few hours each time."

The three sat quiet at the table as Jacob turned it all over in his mind. The banker broke a biscuit open and slathered jam on it, a slight smile playing along the corners of his eyes. He watched as Jacob turned the thought over and around in his head.

I've thought so many times that I would like to have a voice in how things should be done in Brookside and now I would have. It's during planting season and harvest that I'm so very busy. "I don't really know anything about how government works, Mr. Dudley. I'm not sure I'm qualified for such a position."

"Nobody knows until they get involved, sir. We have a community that has just gone through some serious problems. One commissioner, involved in fraud and dead because of it. A county assessor involved in the same illegal scheme and dead because of it. And our territorial judge dead because of it. We need a man with deep seated personal ethics and a strong sense of personal responsibility to help keep things running properly. You're that man, Jacob Hoagland."

Jacob got up from the table and walked around the generous kitchen, wondering how all of this could possibly come about. *The worst year ever, last year. Losing our little girl. On the other hand, new land to work. old land in good condition, and a boy growing faster than our crops. Could I do this? Martha's expecting and will need lots of help this coming summer. Lucas is willing to work harder than any boy I've ever known but he's so young. Needs to learn so much about what we do.*

"I need a little more convincing, Commissioner Dudley." Jacob sat back down and took Martha's hand. "My first priority is my family and then my farm. I'm not sure there's room for a third priority, sir."

"Are you aware of a letter your wife wrote to the commission? About the need for a school?" Jacob smiled and nodded to Martha who ducked her head.

"I knew about thoughts along those lines. You actually wrote a letter to the commission?" He asked and she nodded, her cheeks bright red. She sat still, giving the table top a good look.

"This horrible ordeal we just went through," Commissioner Dudley continued, "with people being killed, tax and land schemes perpetrated by our own leaders, has proved to me that Constable Kennedy needs a deputy. He's done far more than one man should have to do.

"This community needs the kind of leadership that a man like you would bring. Think about it, Hoagland, a growing community, one you have sunk your roots deeply into, and you helping it grow."

"You're awfully convincing, sir," Jacob said. "How

would all this be put together? I wouldn't just walk in the door and say I'm a commissioner, now, would I?"

Dudley smiled, caught the smile on Martha's face, and reached for the coffee pot. "Actually it would almost be like that. The meetings are on the first and third Wednesday of each month, as you well know, so at the next meeting, when you present yourself, you will be sworn in and take your seat. As chairman, I'll do the swearing in."

He saw the grim look on Jacob's face and the wide smile on Martha's. "And, Martha, I'm sure you would like to be there to hold the bible for us."

"You're a nasty man, Commissioner," Jacob said. He had to chuckle and reached out to take Martha's hand again. "I'm still not convinced but it appears as though I'm outnumbered and probably out-foxed too. Leave me everything I'll need to know and I'll be at the next meeting."

"I'm not the one to usually do this," Martha said, "but I think the two of you need to toast each other with a spot of brandy." She went to a cabinet and got an earthen jug of Oregon brandy and two glasses. "Two fine gentlemen need to have a gentle drink to settle the question."

CHAPTER 33

"Is there something we're missing, Constable?" Oscar Levant asked. The two men were sitting at a table in Murphy's Inn and Tavern. "Was Sven Olsen the brains behind this entire criminal scheme?"

"He took advantage of the scheme, I think," Kennedy said. "Because Judge Petrini depended so heavily on him, he jumped at the opportunity. He was skillful at manipulating people to begin with and because of distances between where the various players operated and lack of communication, he became the head man without any of the others recognizing it."

Levant nodded, fully understanding it took days for a missive to be sent from Brookside to Oregon City. It was that immense amount of time that allowed Sven Olsen to assume his leadership position.

"You don't think there's another person involved?" Levant had a worried look on his face. "Olsen doesn't strike me as being capable of leading a scheme of this magnitude." He drained his brandy and called Murphy down for some more.

"No, Inspector, I don't. Gutenberger and Petrini put

together the liquor fraud scheme, and Gutenberger and Creighton put together the land fraud scheme. If Petrini hadn't got greedy Olsen would have never had the opportunity he had to literally take over. I really don't think anyone else is involved. Olsen managed to kill off any who might have been."

Kennedy let his mind think again on what he just said. "Yes, Inspector, it was Petrini who first started skimming money from the liquor sales, and it was Olsen who gave him up. Remember, Olsen didn't raise the alarm about Petrini not showing up at the courthouse until two days had gone by giving Smith all the time he needed to get rid of bloody clothes. Once Petrini was out of the picture, he was able to create the myth that Smith and Gutenberger had to communicate through him."

"For such a small little village, Brookside certainly had its share of criminal activity," Levant chuckled. "There are those in Oregon City who are about to be rousted out. All the names and their positions within the schemes are on paper thanks to that skinny little court clerk. I'll be leaving for Oregon City soon, Kennedy. For what it's worth, you need a deputy."

"I've mentioned it a time or two. Mr. Walling would certainly fill the bill. Judge Anderson will be here this week, filling in until we elect a new one. Only a few left alive but they will face Anderson soon. Sure you won't stay for that?"

"I believe I will," Levant said. "Yes, I believe I will."

A LONE RIDER PULLED HIS HORSE UP IN FRONT OF THE Thorndyke Farm and Implement building before ten o'clock the following morning. He carried a goodly amount of mud from the trail as he dismounted and walked into the large store. "I have a message for Ben Thorndyke," he said. "I've just arrived from Oregon City."

"Follow me, sir," the clerk said and led the visitor through the store and across the meadow to Thorndyke's log cabin office. "A visitor from Oregon City, sir," the clerk said, leading the man in.

"Good," Thorndyke said, getting up from the large chair in front of the fire. "Bring us some good news from the capitol, I hope? We could use some good news around these old parts."

"The governor and his party are about four hours behind me, Mr. Thorndyke. He plans to spend a week on more in Brookside and wishes for you to be available on his arrival." The messenger handed a sealed envelope to Thorndyke, bowed, and stood as if waiting for an answer.

"Tell Governor Raymond I'll have quarters for him at Murphy's Inn and will be at his service. What a wonderful surprise. Thank you, sir." The messenger turned and left. Ben Thorndyke sat at his desk and opened the letter.

"Well, well," he muttered, putting the note down. "Our fine governor will be sitting in the courtroom when Gutenberger and Olsen face lady justice. Showtime," he laughed and made for the main building to alert his wife. then it was time for a visit with Murphy O'Reilly.

Spring was evident everywhere he looked as he made the short walk to Murphy's. "Tell Mrs. O'Reilly her favorite customer will be eating at the family table tonight," Ben said. "Governor Raymond will be in town in just a few hours."

"The missus will be glad to see Henry again. He's as

full of it as Tobias Kennedy, I say, but she's taken with the man's smooth talking. It's been some time since he's paid us a visit."

"It's that smooth talking that made him such a fine salesman for my companies, Murphy. Don't know how many are with him but I told him you'd put him up. We'll have quite a show for him in that old courtroom."

"I've got room for the governor but if he's brought a lot of people, they'll have to fend for themselves. This town is full up, I think. Everyone from miles around coming to watch the fireworks at the courthouse. What's your call, Ben? Think they'll hang Olsen?"

"Well, Murph, let's look at it. Smith did the killing of Petrini and Shelley, not Olsen. Old Slack-jaw, all he did was try to burn down Kennedy's house. Now, back to Olsen," Thorndyke said. "Kennedy is sure Olsen killed Peabody but hasn't filed charges yet. No, no hanging I'm sure, but Gutenberger and Olsen will spend some time in prison, that's for sure. A lot of dead people, though. Ah, here's Kennedy now. Good morning to you, Constable."

"And to you, Ben. Morning Murph, how about a brandy to get my blood flowing in the right direction. A lot of faces out there I've not seen before, you got a sale going on, Ben?"

Thorndyke laughed right out. "No, Toby, they're here for the big show you'll be putting on at the courthouse. Is Claude Atkins up to a trial like this? Man needs to retire and move to west Texas or someplace hot and dry."

"No forces around here strong enough to tear him away from his timber business, Ben. Sylvia, the doctor, me, we've all told him what you just said and all he does is ramble on about the virtues of fir trees. He doesn't mention the silver they bring in, though." He laughed and grabbed his glass.

"He has help coming, though," Kennedy continued. "He got a note that the Territorial Attorney General is sending a couple of attorneys to aid the gentleman. Should be coming in today."

"Things are starting to make sense, eh Murphy?" Thorndyke chuckled. "The governor is expected in shortly as well, Kennedy. Those attorneys have quite an escort. What's Atkins' call on how they'll charge Olsen? I would assume most of the charges against Gutenberger will emanate from Oregon City, not locally." Thorndyke motioned for Murphy to refill all the glasses.

"Be good to see Henry again. He doesn't get down this way often enough. Olsen and Gutenberger will face relatively simple charges of evading import taxes, selling illegal liquor because of the failure to pay the tax, and conspiracy to evade the taxes." He shook his head and sipped his brandy.

"There is no one alive to charge with the violent deaths of Peabody, Petrini, and Shelley," the constable said.

"I was under the impression that it was Olsen who killed Peabody, Constable. What's changed here?" Thorndyke said.

"Nothing's changed, Ben, it's simply there is no evidence that he did, only conjecture at this point. I haven't one single piece of evidence that says Olsen killed Commissioner Peabody. Believe me, I've taken that office apart, Olsen's court clerk office, and Olsen's house, and there is nothing that I can offer the court."

"What would it take, Toby?" Murphy asked.

"The knife," Kennedy said. "for one. If I could tie the knife to the man." He shook his head and looked back and forth at the men. "No one was there, in the building, when Peabody was killed except he and the killer. No witnesses, nothing left behind. Unless I can find something in the next couple of days, the man won't be charged with murder."

Kennedy stopped talking, stared at the bottles behind Murphy with a blank expression on his face. "Excuse me, gentlemen, I've got to find Inspector Levant." He put his half empty glass on the bar and walked out the door.

"That's something you'll not see again in this lifetime, Ben Thorndyke. Tobias Kennedy leaving a half-filled glass."

CHAPTER 34

"There you are," Kennedy said. "I have half the town looking for you." Oscar Levant was in Kennedy's office writing. "We need to take a ride out Turkey Run Road. I'll explain on the way." They dashed out and jumped in the buggy since it was already harnessed and Kennedy drove them out at a strong trot. "We'll be looking for the knife that was used to kill Commissioner Peabody. Find it, bloody clothing, anything related to Peabody's office, and we hang one Sven Olsen," Kennedy said, giving his horse another quick switch on the back side.

"Didn't see anything like that when we found all that gold, but then, we weren't looking for it. Take that cabin apart first and then the cave, eh?" Levant said. "Not many places in the cabin to hide anything but one could hide a bloody knife anywhere in that cave."

Kennedy drove the buggy right up to the cabin door and the men climbed out. "Doesn't look like anyone's been here since we moved that gold," Kennedy said. They walked in and started searching along the walls, under every piece of furniture, behind clothing hanging from pegs and found nothing. Levant even opened the door of the cast iron stove and rustled his fingers through the ash.

"Glad we tore most of those brambles from the cave entrance," Levant said. "I'm still bleeding in a couple of places."

The cave search was far more extensive and the only thing they came up with was a shirt that appeared to be ripped and possibly stained with blood. "Even if it fits him, he can say he's never seen it before," Levant said.

Kennedy walked out of the cave entrance and into the sun, turning the shirt up, down, and around, giving every square inch of fabric a good look-see. "Maybe not, Inspector. The letters SO are embroidered into the back collar. We know Peabody put up a fight before dying, the shirt is ripped and bloody, and has these markings. It's good evidence."

"I have an idea, Constable. Let's walk around that corral. You walk the outside perimeter, from a good ten feet or more, and I'll walk inside the fence."

Kennedy smiled, rolled the shirt up and tucked it on the seat of the buggy. The bushes outside the corral fence were cleared back about two feet from the fence and Kennedy slowly made his way through the brush and tall grass looking back and forth with each step.

If we find a blood stained knife it will hammer down the lid to Olsen's coffin. If he stepped down from his horse, knew he had to get rid of the knife, where would he throw it? Kennedy stood up and looked all around the corral. *Over the top and behind the open stall is where I'd throw it.*

He continued going through the brush and got even more intense as he made his way behind the thrown-together stall. *Nothing. We need to find that knife. The shirt is good evidence, but that knife is the hangman.*

"I got nothing," Levant said. "You had the right idea, and we do have the shirt."

"Where would you chuck it?"

"I'd be more apt to hide it, I think," the inspector said. "Let's walk around that cabin again."

They were halfway around, along the south wall and Levant stopped, knelt down, and shoved a large rock aside. "Look at the size of that hole, Mr. Kennedy. Big enough for a skinny man like Olsen to crawl in." Levant knew he was too big and Kennedy would never fit.

Kennedy walked up to the wall and gave it a mighty kick sending kindling flying. Two more kicks and either man could crawl under the cabin with ease. Kennedy went first and yelped after just barely getting under. "Got it," he said. Then laughed. "Or it got me." He crawled out with the knife showing a spot of blood where he put his hand down on the sharp blade.

"That and the shirt will hang Mr. Olsen," Levant said. "Let's get these safely tucked away in your office and pay your friend Murphy a little visit, eh?"

"How are we going to prove this is Olsen's knife?" Kennedy had only been thinking of finding a bloody knife, not proving it was Olsen's. He turned it over a time or two, almost squinting, trying to find an owner's mark, as on a tool.

Using the shirt and what he knew of Olsen, Kennedy was sure there would be an owner's mark of some kind on the knife. The man marked everything in the office, and monogrammed his shirts, surely he would mark a good knife. "There it is," he said. "Look, Levant. On the tang, SO, the same as the shirt."

"Do we have anything else marked SO that we can use to prove that's how Olsen marked his belongings?"

"Indeed we do," Kennedy smiled. "That's how he

marked his papers, books, and even some objects I found in his house. We've got him good."

It was almost a homecoming for a local hero when Oregon Territorial Governor Henry Raymond led his procession into town. As a top salesman for Ben Thorndyke, Raymond was always open and friendly with everyone. As a politician, it might seem as though nothing had changed. People recognized the affable man and waved, yelled hello, and the governor was quick to respond in kind. A small crowd followed the procession to Murphy's Inn and Tavern.

"We've got you set up, Henry and the missus can't wait to see you,"

"Hello, Murphy. You've put on a pound or two, my friend." The governor stood at the bar and spent some time looking the place over. "I've missed this place, Murph. Missed your wife's cooking, and discussions at the family table. You still short pouring?"

"Ha! I've never shorted a man in my life," Murphy said. "Well, maybe a time or two," He laughed. "Never you, though."

"Ah, Thorndyke, I thought I'd missed you," Raymond said. "I've no real agenda on this visit. I'll be in the court-room for some of the trial, but I also want to make sure Judge Adamson follows through on the Creighton boy's case. My order needs to be finalized by the court and that boy needs to be institutionalized."

"Mrs. Creighton will be most pleased to hear that, Governor. I understand you brought some attorneys from the Attorney General's office to help with the proceedings." Raymond nodded and Thorndyke contin-ued. "There won't be much action in the courtroom, I'm afraid. Of an amazing number of people involved in these frauds and murders, only two suspects remain alive."

"It's the land fraud portion that has my attention, Ben. We keep hearing about great numbers of people moving across those broad plains out there," and he waved his hands as if taking in the entire continent, "wanting to come to Oregon Territory. I want our land commissioners to be as honest as the sunrise. Creighton and Gutenberger have cast doubts on our policies and that needs to be rectified."

"We hear about the possibility of some people, territorial officials, who worked with Gutenberger and Creighton. Are those rumors true?" Thorndyke asked.

"We have three men in custody, Ben. I doubt if there are more. Your constable, Kennedy, has done a fine job down here. Have you found replacements for the Brookside officials who were killed? The county needs to be fully functional."

"We're about to have a new county commissioner. I think you've met him, Jacob Hoagland. He's an upstanding citizen."

"Hoagland," the governor said. "Yes, has that property in the foothills. Hard worker. Lovely wife as I recall. How about the assessor? Damn thief. Got a replacement?"

"Commissioners will appoint one to serve until the next election. I assume," Ben said, "that you'll appoint a new judge for us."

"First thing on my calendar when I get back. Have several names to look at. This is such a big territory, from the continental divide to the Pacific Ocean, Ben. It's a rich country, too, for ranching and farming. My God, Ben if you drop a seed you better step aside for that plant will grow fast enough to knock you down." He laughed loud and strong along with those at the bar.

"You're a natural politician, Henry, and just as good as when you were a salesman." Thorndyke said.

"ARE YOU SURE THIS IS FOR ME?" IRENE CREIGHTON answered a loud knock on her new door and faced one of the clerks from Thorndyke's Emporium. "It looks awfully official."

"Mr. Thorndyke asked me to deliver it personally, Ma'am, and to wait for an answer."

"All right, then, come in and we'll go to the kitchen. Like a cup of coffee?" She led the young man through the house and into the kitchen where Carrie was at the table reading. "Please, sit down and I'll get us a cup. My goodness, this just looks so official." She held the envelope for another few seconds before putting it down and going to the stove.

She fought off the fear that this had something to do with Jeremy. She knew she had to open the letter, knew someone was waiting for her answer, but her trembling fingers wouldn't cooperate. She finally got it torn open and let out a gasp when she saw the signature.

The governor wrote me a personal note? She read it over quickly, smiled at the clerk, motioned Carrie to come over and see. "It's from Governor Raymond, honey. Look. He wants me to join him for supper with Ben Thorndyke and his wife. Oh, my, but," and she found herself speechless.

Carrie can't be left alone but I certainly can't turn the governor down. What should I tell this young man? Her mind was a whirl-a-gig of activity as she sat drumming her fingers on the table. "Let me get paper and ink," she said, getting up and walking into what once was Creighton's little office, now headquarters for Creighton Book-keeping Service.

I must go. This is not something I would miss no matter what. I'll find a way to take care of Carrie. She fought off the shakes, penned a quick letter of acceptance and handed it to the clerk.

"Mr. Thorndyke said to tell you that Carrie should also come as the children will have their supper alone but with supervision." The clerk started to get up from the table.

"You knew what was in the letter?" Irene asked.

"I was standing next to the governor when he wrote the letter. He read it out loud to make sure it was right. Yes, Ma'am, I was there."

"Is he as nice as everyone says?"

"Gave me a silver dollar to deliver this. He's pretty nice," the clerk said. "Never had one of these before. Goodbye."

CHAPTER 35

The Thorndyke carriage showed up at seven o'clock and Irene and Carrie were driven to the Thorndyke home for supper with the governor. The ladies were in their finest and Carrie was full of a thousand questions that Irene couldn't answer. Why were they having supper with the governor? Was this because of Jeremy? Are you in trouble Mama?

After saying, "I don't know," for the one hundredth time, she finally told Carrie she would have to wait and find out. "Mr. Thorndyke and Governor Raymond are personal friends, sweetheart, and I don't know the answers to your questions. Just remember to mind your manners and be the perfect little lady you always are."

The Thorndyke home was ablaze with light. Irene was almost frightened at the number of people who were there. Dignitaries who accompanied the governor from Oregon City, County officials, and long time Brookside friends were there. Carrie was escorted to where multitudes of children were, and Irene was taken straight to Governor Raymond.

"Mrs. Creighton," he said, taking her hand and

bowing slightly. "I'm so pleased to meet you. Ben tells me you're the finest bookkeeper he's ever known. We might want you in our territorial offices," he chuckled.

"I want to get right to the point, Ma'am. Judge Adamson has set aside the findings of Judge Petrini and there will be a hearing before him dealing with your son, Jeremy. The charges will remain, and Adamson assures me your son will most likely have to spend several years incarcerated at the Boy's Farm. I'm terribly sorry you had to face these awkward and anxious times."

All Irene could say was thank you as tears rolled down her bright red cheeks. "I'm sorry, Governor, but I can't hold them back." He handed her his handkerchief and gently patted her on the back.

"Everything all right here?" Ben Thorndyke said. "Good heavens, Henry, what have you done?" Thorndyke had a big smile on his face.

"I gave her the good news, Ben. It's been a long time coming, I'm afraid. Ah," the governor said. "Here's another man I've been looking forward to meeting. Please, Ben, introduce us."

"With pleasure, sir. Jacob, please say hello to Governor Raymond. Henry, meet the new Brookside County Commissioner Jacob Hoagland. And this is the lovely Mrs. Hoagland."

"Did you know the governor came in while we were having our meal, Mama? Isn't that exciting? The governor of Oregon Territory sat down with us for almost ten minutes. I've never met a governor before." Carrie Creighton was more excited than Irene had ever seen the girl.

"He's the first governor I've ever met, too, honey. He

gave us some good news, too. Your brother will not be moving back into this house. I hope that whatever happens to him is best for him, even if it isn't nice to think about. He'll never hurt you again, Carrie. Never."

"Lucas said we're supposed to go to their farm this Sunday. Is that right? I like him."

"He's a good boy. Yes, Sunday supper with the Hoagland's again. I like that idea, too. First there's supper with the governor then supper with the county commissioner. Do you suppose the president will be sending an invitation soon?"

"You're funny, Mama."

It wasn't that long ago, she thought, *that the idea of just being out in public was denied to us by Ed Creighton and now we're dining with the governor, taking our buggy for rides through beautiful country, and enjoying friendships with real people. There really are good people in the world, particularly here in Brookside.*

"WELL, INSPECTOR, YOU HAVE A GOOD RIDE BACK TO Oregon City. You'll always be welcome here," Constable Kennedy said. They were standing outside the courthouse on a beautiful spring morning. Levant was escorting John Gutenberger to the territorial prison instead of riding back with Governor Raymond and his entourage following a three-day trial.

"It was an interesting time, Constable. Most interesting. Tell Murphy I'll miss his wife's fine food." Gutenberger was in an iron cage in the back of a wagon driven by a couple of loggers hired by the inspector. "I'm not sure that ten years at hard labor was enough, considering the problems this man created, but I'm also sure he probably won't live through it."

"Well, we know Olsen won't," Kennedy chuckled. "I guess you're right getting Gutenberger off to prison quickly. The hanging will be day after tomorrow at sunrise. They're always gruesome. Let me know how those territorial officers do in their trials."

"Got everyone out of town, finally," Murphy said when Kennedy walked in. "Maybe we can get back to being a nice quiet little frontier village, eh?"

"Doubtful, Murph. We still have three lumber companies, two lumber mills, one flour mill, and that new distillery operating. Brookside started out as a farming village but has never been a quiet little frontier village. Not since I've been here."

"At least the commissioners gave you Mr. Walling."

"Yes, they did. You can tell Mrs. O'Reilly that she'll be safe in her warm kitchen. Jacob Hoagland's going to be a fine commissioner, too, I think. He's got them talking about creating a real school for the children. Did you ever go to school, Murph?"

"Aye, Laddie, that I did. Left after the third year when my pop said I knew enough. You?"

"Mother taught me to read and do my numbers. Nope, never been in a school. I think it's a good idea, though. I do. I think there must be a lot of things I don't know anything about. Might want to sit in sometime."

"Have a taste of the old country, Constable, the streets are safe for the time being."

TAKE A LOOK AT NAME'S
CORCORAN:A TERRENCE CORCORAN
WESTERN BOOK ONE

Terrence Corcoran carried a badge in Virginia City, Nevada until one day, in a drunken stupor, he shot the sheriff. Now he's returning to the Comstock looking to get his badge back and stumbles into a conspiracy that might put the sheriff, district attorney, and others in jail for a long time. A lovely working girl is brutally murdered, a Hungarian duke wants a Wells Fargo gold shipment, and the sheriff rehires him after first kicking him in a most tender spot. Corcoran was born on the ship bringing his family to this country, ran away to the frontier at an early age and brings his ideas of the old country and knowledge learned of the west to whatever mess he finds himself in. He's carried a badge, found himself in jail, and stands four-square for right, honor, and truth. You gotta love the guy.

AVAILABLE NOW

ABOUT THE AUTHOR

Reno, Nevada novelist, Johnny Gunn, is retired from a long career in journalism. He has worked in print, broadcast, and Internet, including a stint as publisher and editor of the Virginia City Legend. These days, Gunn spends most of his time writing novel length fiction, concentrating on the western genre. Or, you can find him down by the Truckee River with a fly rod in hand.

"It's been a wonderful life. I was born in Santa Cruz, California, on the north shore of fabled Monterey Bay. When I was fourteen, that would have been 1953, we moved to Guam and I went through my high school years living in a tropical paradise. I learned to scuba dive from a WWII Navy Frogman, learned to fly from a WWII combat pilot (by dad), but I knew how to fish long before I moved to Guam.

"I spent time on the Island of Truk, which during WWII was a huge Japanese naval base, and dived in the lagoon. Massive U.S. air strikes sunk thousands of tons of Japanese naval craft, and it was more than exciting to dive on those wrecks. In the Palau Islands, near Koror, I also dived on Japanese aircraft that had been shot down into the lagoons.

"My own service time consisted of my defending you from Puerto Rico during the Cuban Missile Crisis. Seems as though I couldn't get away from tropical paradise. The diving was good but the fishing was splendid.

"I've been living in Nevada since 1963, following my service time with the army. You'd have to hunt hard and long to find a spot in the Silver State that I haven't visited, and you'll find many of those spots in my stories. I've caught ten and eleven pound trout at Pyramid Lake and caught ten inch brook trout that were fully mature and would take you arm right out of the socket with their strikes.

"Besides Virginia City, home of the fabled Comstock Lode, I've lived in Manhattan, Nevada. There were 120 of us at the time. I spent some time in Silver Peak, another very small community, and our home now is in an area called Cold Springs. There's a casino here called Border Town. The state line separating Nevada and California runs right through it. We can ride our horse a few hundred yards and be in California, right along the eastern flank of the Sierra Nevada.

"We have a small hobby farm and raise a considerable amount of our own food. Cold Springs is about twenty miles north of Reno. We raise chickens for meat and eggs, and large New Zealand White rabbits for their meat. We raise the standard New Zealand which are large, but there are also Giant New Zealand rabbits. We haven't gotten into them. The goat provides milk and young ones for their meat.

"My lovely wife says the little hobby farm keeps me out of trouble, and then snickers and says, maybe not. If you're in our area, stop in, I always need help cleaning corrals."